MISS RIDDELL AND THE HEIRESS

AN AMATEUR FEMALE SLEUTH HISTORICAL
COZY MYSTERY

P.C. JAMES

LITHGOW, BLUE MOUNTAINS. NSW, AUSTRALIA – 1977

P auline Riddell looked around the boardroom table at the assembled company as the chairman called the meeting to order before saying, "I don't need to tell you why we're here."

There was no response to this for everyone did indeed know why they were here. The forensic audit team sent from the head office in England was to present its findings today. Rumors of what those findings were had been circulating for days.

"You'll notice our finance director isn't present," the chairman continued. "The reason for that will become clear when you hear the report, but I will tell you right now that he was arrested this morning at Sydney Airport as he and his family were preparing to board an international flight." He paused to give the board members time to grasp the full weight of his words before continuing, "The chief accountant is also being held by the police and being questioned as to how much he knew. It's a sorry state of affairs and one I feel I should have seen but I didn't. Consequently, I've tendered my resignation to the board of our head office;

they, however, have asked me to stay on until a replacement can be found."

There was some murmuring and shuffling among the board members and, Pauline was pleased to see, some shamed faces among them. After all, what were a company's board members for if not to ensure financial and other irregularities did not take place?

The chairman continued, "Now, I think you've all met the audit team members, Mr. Entwhistle and Miss Riddell, so I'll ask them to walk us through the report and its findings."

The two auditors began circulating the slim report around the table until everyone had a copy.

"I shall talk to the general conclusions and recommendations," Entwhistle said, "and Miss Riddell will take us through the research, analysis, and findings. Are there any questions before we begin?"

There were none and the meeting began.

Afterwards, as she and Entwhistle were packing to leave, Pauline took stock of her trip. They'd been in Australia three weeks but hadn't seen anything other than offices and hotel rooms. In theory, they were both supposed to return to England tomorrow to write up their overseas trip report and be available for another assignment, but she decided she needed a break. She might never be in Australia again and she hadn't even seen a kangaroo in the whole time she'd been here.

"Colin," she said, addressing her fellow auditor, "I'm staying on for a few days. I need a vacation."

"The boss won't like it," Entwhistle said.

"I won't be long," Pauline replied. "A week's holiday, that's all. I want to see a wombat."

"What's a wombat?"

"Some kind of animal," Pauline said. "I don't know really."

"We have zoos full of animals, Pauline," Entwhistle said. "You can see them at home."

"Tell him I'll be at work a week on Monday without fail," Pauline said.

Entwhistle shook his head. "Not a chance," he said. "You call and tell him while I'm still in the air over the Indian Ocean. I don't want to be even close by when he hears that."

"He works himself, and us, too hard," Pauline said. "It's bad for his nerves and his temper."

"Tell him that too," Entwhistle said. "You should be safe calling it in from here."

AFTER DROPPING Entwhistle at Sydney Airport, Pauline jumped back into their rented car and headed out to explore some of Australia's spectacular scenery and unique wildlife. Her plan was simple, tour the Blue Mountains and its surroundings and finish the week back in Sydney to see where modern Australia began.

At the age of forty-four, and with many single vacations behind her, Pauline had no problem setting out on her own through the mountain trails that led to waterfalls or unusual rockfalls. Sometimes, however, she still couldn't help feeling a companion would make the experience more enjoyable. After all, her own appreciation of the Three Sisters at Katoomba, or the Zig-Zag Railway nearby, were satisfying but not complete. Australia's brightly colored birdlife alone would have been enough for hours of conversation.

Her first three weeks of the trip, spent entirely indoors studying files, accounts, and folders, were forgotten as she roamed through the dry landscape under a burning sun in a clear blue sky. She'd read Australia was the driest inhabited continent and she could believe it. This was winter and she hadn't seen or heard even a drop of rain the whole time. Much of the vegetation she walked on was brown, crisp, and crackled underfoot. Only where thin streams meandered through the forest floor or poured over the plateau edge in rainbow-creating falls, was the land green. It was stunning to her senses. How it felt to those first settlers from rainy Britain two hundred years ago, she couldn't imagine. Nor could she imagine what they felt when they saw the wildlife, which was totally alien to her and no doubt to their European upbringing. Lots of the local wildlife were gorgeous furry bundles: kangaroos, wallabies, and their related species. Others were just cute, like echidnas. But the fruit bats, snakes, and spiders were rather frightening. Fortunately, she rarely saw those on her walks.

Too soon, her time was up, and she headed back down the narrow road through the mountains bound for Sydney and its city life. Her research into the city had told her to stay somewhere near The Rocks, the city's starting point, where she would see the early buildings of the port and be well placed for all the sightseeing she wanted to do. She could walk to Circular Quay where ferries and tour boats took locals and sightseers to all the principal locations. She could even walk to the newest and most controversial of the attractions, the Sydney Opera House. She could also walk across Sydney's famous Harbour Bridge, so well-known in her own north-eastern England, and admire the vast, sheltered bay that had attracted people for centuries. A ferry would take her to Taronga Zoo where she hoped she could finally see the wombat, as none had made an appearance during any of her walkabouts through the, admittedly now too well-traveled, Blue Mountain trails.

Her first days in Sydney were spent in the Opera House and the Natural History Museum, which had she visited it at the start might have had her flying straight home because the list of Australia's poisonous creatures was seemingly never-ending. By comparison, her time wandering among the Botanical Gardens, with its flock of fruit bats hanging from the highest trees, was tame. Her time on the beach at Botany Bay, famous in the British folk songs she remembered, and Manly Beach, where the surfers and lifeguards were sadly not in evidence because it was winter, was instructive. The air and water were both warmer than her childhood summer days on a packed beach at Scarborough and yet the beaches were empty. It was hard for Pauline to appreciate that Australians actually thought these pleasant, sunny, warm days were cold. Her final morning she spent on the water, touring the bay from a Captain Cook Tours boat, and in the afternoon, she took the ferry across to the Zoo, which covered much of the slopes on the opposite side of the bay from the city.

2

SYDNEY, NSW, AUSTRALIA – NOVEMBER 1977

Walking around Taronga Zoo took longer than she'd expected. After an hour, with much of the zoo unexplored, she sat down at the cafeteria for a pot of tea and a lamington cake. She was hardly settled when she noticed a woman who was vaguely familiar hovering nearby. Pauline broke off a piece of her lamington cake and watched her approach. Now she was closer, Pauline remembered the woman had been on the same morning Captain Cook Cruise around the harbor and bay with her and even then, she'd seemed to take a special interest in Pauline. Pauline wracked her brain to make a connection between the woman and the many new people she'd met since arriving in Australia only four weeks earlier. She couldn't think of anyone she'd met that resembled the woman, who was still circling closer looking unable to decide whether to speak or leave.

She was dressed for a vacation and that alone set her apart from the other Australians all around who were in 'winter' clothes, this being the depths of Sydney's winter season. Pauline was in her spring clothes; for to a northern

Englishwoman, an Australian winter was more like a summer's day. But this mysterious and conflicted stranger was also in her summery clothes of a flower-printed dress and bare legs, though with a light, fawn coat over her arm.

Pauline took a sip of tea and continued nibbling her cake while she waited for the woman to make up her mind. Lamington cake, a sponge cube rolled in chocolate and shredded coconut, Pauline finally decided, was interesting, but in the end, just sponge cake. In Pauline's mind, pastries were always better than cakes. The zoo café was busy with families enjoying snacks in the bright sunshine and under the clear blue sky that hadn't changed since she'd arrived in Australia. Those crowds, however, made it hard for Pauline to always keep the woman in sight.

She could see the woman was attractive, but somewhat unusually, wore no jewelry to enhance her face, neck, or arms. Her honey-blonde hair was fashionably cut but not in the hideous modern styles that came from watching too much television or movies. Pauline guessed she was about thirty, though her manner was almost that of a socially awkward teenager. Her hovering wasn't threatening but even if it had been, Pauline wouldn't have been concerned. They were evenly matched in height and weight and Pauline, when the dangers of her forays into crime solving had become too apparent, had taken lessons in self defense. She saw herself very much in the mold of Mrs. Emma Peel in that silly television show, The Avengers, which had been so popular in the Sixties. Though she fully recognized and disapproved of the nonsense it showed, she'd gone ahead and taken lessons. While she knew even a trained woman like herself couldn't win a fight against a violent, aggressive man, let alone the kind of supposedly trained agents Mrs. Peel was always besting in fights, it was enough to know that the element of surprise early in a fight could turn out in her favor.

Just as Pauline was thinking of leaving the small table, the woman came to a decision and approached her directly.

"Excuse me," she said. "Can I talk to you for a moment?"

She spoke English with an Australian accent, Pauline noticed, not Australian English. Perhaps she was a newcomer who was just beginning to settle in.

"Of course," Pauline said, gesturing to the seat at the opposite side of the small table.

"You don't know me," the woman said abruptly and stopped.

"Well, we can correct that at once," Pauline said. "I'm Pauline Riddell." She held out her hand.

The woman took Pauline's hand and shook it. Her hand was soft but her handshake firm. Despite her initial suspicions, Pauline felt herself thawing.

"Alexandra Wade," she said, "but I prefer just plain Alex." She stopped speaking abruptly again but this time it seemed less odd because she was settling herself in the chair Pauline had offered.

Pauline decided to wait it out. The woman wanted to talk, that was clear, but she'd have to decide to do so in her own time. After all, Pauline was flying home tomorrow and couldn't help anyone here. She mentally shook herself. No one here knew she was Miss Riddell, fighter for justice and righter of wrongs, as her journalist friend Poppy had once described her in a newspaper article. She smiled to herself. Poppy's words from long ago and far away, while silly, did come to mind often, which was of course pride and therefore a failing she did her best to suppress.

"You talked about Whalley to the people on the boat this morning," Alexandra said at last.

For a moment, Pauline had a mental block, then she remembered, "Oh, yes," she said, "the British couple on the boat told me they were from Manchester before emigrating here. They asked me if I knew Manchester."

Alexandra nodded. "Then you said you lived in Whalley."

"I do now," Pauline said. "I moved there some months ago. Why? Do you know it?"

"I've never been there but I know of it," Alex said. "My mum said we were descendants of a noble family from near there." She paused, then continued. "Do you know a village called Ashton de Cheney?"

"No," Pauline said slowly, "but I'm not a local in the area. As I said, I only moved there a few months ago. Do you live in Sydney? It's a beautiful city."

"No," Alex said, "I was born and raised in Victoria. Wadeville. It's a tiny place about a hundred miles inland from Melbourne."

"I've heard Melbourne is a beautiful city too," Pauline said.

"I wouldn't know," Alex said, "apart from the airport, I've never been there."

"Never?" Pauline asked.

"We never got off the station much when I was a kid," Alex said. "Then when Dad took off, and we lost the farm and had to move into town, Mum and I couldn't afford to go anywhere."

"I'm sorry," Pauline said. "Still, the country around there must be beautiful so you can't have missed much growing up."

"It is pretty around the town," Alex agreed. "Living there, you forget. It takes a stranger to remind you of things sometimes."

"That's very true," Pauline said. "Visitors came to where I grew up all the time and it was a long time before I could see the moors as they saw them."

"My difficulty is different." Alex said. "The country I grew up in is beautiful but our poverty, after Dad left, makes me hate it."

"I'm sorry to hear that," Pauline said, though wondering what any of this had to do with her. "It must have been very hard."

Alex shook her head. "You don't understand, I'm not explaining it well. It was a poverty of mind more than of the body, and it was made worse by my mother's belief we were 'quality', as she called it, and we had to keep ourselves above our neighbors."

Pauline was beginning to think the woman wasn't quite right in the head and considered how best to extricate herself from this increasingly worrisome interview.

"It is hard when you're young not to have things others have," Pauline said.

"It wasn't like that," Alex said, almost angrily. "I didn't care about material things. It was the lack of friends, the loneliness – the teasing and bullying at school – which drove me to leave school early and miss out on university."

Pauline frowned. Any moment, she was going to be asked to donate to something, she was sure of it.

Seeing Pauline's expression seemed to sober, Alex said, "You see, I lived all my life in a tiny village of fifty people and hadn't a relative or friend in the whole place. My mother's obsession with being 'aristocracy' kept us apart. People don't like being told they're below you on some idiotic social scale from a far-away country."

"I can see how that would cause friction," Pauline agreed, and she could. Alex's mother must have been deranged to give herself airs and graces in a land as egalitarian as Australia prided itself on being.

"Friction doesn't begin to describe it," Alex said, her temper clearly rising again. "When I was a teenager, the other kids were always having crushes on each other, going out, falling out. Nobody wanted me. Mother would say 'a pretty girl like you will soon get a good husband, not one of these local yokels' but she didn't have to run home from school to stop the yokels pawing her, not because they were attracted to me but because they wanted to hurt and humiliate me. Mother's obsession was a nightmare I lived with until..." she stopped.

"Until?" Pauline said, feeling the woman was getting to the point at last.

"She died, about a month ago."

"Oh, I am sorry," Pauline said. Did the woman just want a shoulder to cry on? Pauline hoped not for she wasn't the shoulder-crying-on sort.

The silence grew as Alex clearly tried to recover her thoughts and feelings.

"I have no one, you see, or not really," she said at last, "and I don't like where I live so I thought I'd make the trip to England to see if what mother said was true."

"I still don't understand why you're telling me this or what it is you hope to learn in England," Pauline said.

"Mother said I'm the rightful heir to the de Cheney estate in a village called Ashton de Cheney near Whalley and one day we'd go back and claim it."

Pauline asked, "Was your mother from Ashton de Cheney?"

Alex shook her head. "No," she said. "That was my real dad, he was the de Cheney. Mum was just a regular girl. They met in the war, but he was killed before I was even born. And so were his parents, by a bomber unloading its bombs. Mum said the Jerry was afraid of all the flak over Liverpool, so he dropped his bombs early and scampered back to Germany. She says it happened a lot. The Jerries were cowardly like that, not like our boys who flew right into the thick of it." Alex paused, then added, "My real father, Jocelyn de Cheney, was a bomber pilot and he was killed over Germany. That may have clouded her judgment."

Pauline smiled; Alex's wryly honest comment confirmed what she'd suspected. Beneath that awkward manner was a more mature woman trying to emerge.

"Perhaps," Pauline said, 'but still I prefer simple national pride to the modern fashion for revisionism."

"I do too," Alex said, "I feel the pilots on both sides were incredibly brave though I never told mother that. She'd have skinned me alive."

"It's always a mistake to run down your enemy," Pauline agreed. "It devalues your victory if you win and humiliates you further if you lose."

"Exactly," Alex said.

"I still don't see why you wanted to speak to me?" Pauline asked. She felt it was time to get to the heart of the issue before her whole afternoon was lost.

"If I'm the rightful heir to the de Cheney estate, or at least I have a claim on it," Alex said, "I'd like to know. Some money would be welcome, of course, though I've a good job now so it isn't just that. Perhaps I have a family who may even be happy to know me."

This story was different, Pauline thought. Since arriving in Australia, she'd heard one or two strange stories about 'back home' but this one was unusual. A missing heiress was straight out of a romance novel, and it quite likely was!

"So why didn't your mother claim the estate for you?"

she asked. "After all, the postal service is very quick and efficient nowadays."

"She said it was because her husband died before his parents did and he never got to pass it on to her," Alex replied. "Presumably the inheritance passed to some other branch of the family."

"That's bad luck," Pauline agreed.

"I think so," Alex said seriously, "but I imagine it happened a lot in history. All those wars and plagues and things."

"Probably it did," Pauline agreed again.

"What would happen if there wasn't another branch of the family?"

"I'm not a lawyer," Pauline said, "and I'm sure it depends on the circumstances, but I'd guess it goes to the British state."

"What if someone claimed it years later?"

"I've no idea," Pauline said. "Probably a successful claimant would inherit but, again I'm guessing, there must be a time period allowed. You couldn't claim too long after the death or the State would have disposed of it. Are you thinking you might have a case?"

"Lately," Alex said slowly, "I've been wondering. Since Mum died, I've been on my own and I thought a trip to England might... you know. Well, you wouldn't because I don't know..." Alex let the sentence dribble away into nothing.

"I'm sorry I can't be more help," Pauline said. 'I really know very little about inheritance law." This wasn't entirely truthful, but Pauline didn't want to give the woman false hopes. She saw Alex nod in thanks, her mind far away.

"I do hope you're able to get the help you need," Pauline

began, gathering her purse and jacket in preparation for
leaving.

"Please," Alex said, "don't go. I only want to know something of where you live and how I might begin my quest for
the truth. Just a few minutes, please?"

Pauline laid her bag and jacket down. It was difficult.
She was torn between her usual desire to help others who
needed help and her equally strong desire to not be
imposed upon.

"Tell me quickly what you want to know," Pauline said,
"and I'll do my best."

"Where is the village? I couldn't find it on the map."

"I'm as puzzled about that as you are," Pauline said. "I've
never heard of it and yet you think it's somewhere near
where I live."

"Well, where is that?"

"In Lancashire, just a few miles north of Manchester,"
Pauline said.

"So, I could fly to London and then take a train to there?"

"Yes, very easily."

"How would I find out about wills and family matters?"

"Do that at Somerset House in London before you travel
north," Pauline said, happier now they were talking prac-
tical matters.

"As easy as that?"

"Research is never quite that easy but that's where you
start," Pauline said.

"Thank you," Alex said, "I had no idea. Could I ask a
favor? It won't take much of your time."

"If I can," Pauline said, wary again.

"If I give you my address, would you find out what you
can about the village and hall of Ashton de Cheney and
send me the details? That way I'd know if there even is such

a place because from what you've said, and my uninformed map reading, there isn't."

"Yes, I think I could do that," Pauline said, making a mental note not to provide a return address on her letter. "It should be a quick and simple history project and I liked doing those at school."

"I always hated history," Alex said. "My life was blighted by history and I couldn't see how it might help anyone to know more of it."

Pauline smiled. "Well, this time it might work out to your benefit. If I find there isn't or wasn't an Ashton de Cheney, you'll be saved the expense of the trip and if I find there was, you may have the opportunity of a family and some additional money. A win-win as we say in business."

"I hope so," Alex said, though it didn't sound hopeful.

Pauline again picked up her bag and coat. "Well, I must be going," she said. "I have to pack for my flight home tomorrow and before I go, I want to see a wombat."

"Can I walk with you?"

"Of course," Pauline said. "Maybe you can tell me more as we walk."

"Yes, of course. Sorry," said Alex, "I'm spoiling your afternoon outing."

"Not at all," Pauline lied. "I can see my wombat and you can tell me more of your mother's story. Something might click with me that would help."

They set off walking toward the 'Australian animals' section of the zoo. Pauline could see Alex was still struggling to articulate what it was she'd hoped to get from approaching her and decided to help her along.

"Perhaps tell me from the beginning," she said. "Where did your mother's story start?"

"It started one night in 1944," Alex said. "I've heard it so many times, I can recite it word for word."

"What was her name, by the way? We can't call her 'Mother' all afternoon."

"Adelaide, but she always went by Adie," Alex said.

"It seemed, even when she was christened, she was destined for Australia," Pauline said, smiling.

"Yes, my step-dad said that in the beginning too," Alex replied. "He told me that when I met him here in Sydney. I came here thinking it would lift me out of the depression that settled on me when Mother died."

"You were going to tell me your mother's story," Pauline reminded her. It seemed highly unlikely from the little she'd heard that Alex would have a claim on anything but maybe there was more that would shed a different light.

"All right, I will," Alex said. "Mother described it in such detail there has to be something in it. It can't have been a story she made up. Anyway, she couldn't have been so cruel to expose me to all the misery for a made-up story."

Pauline hesitated, and then said, "She may just have wanted to keep you to herself, don't you think? People often do strange things, unkind things, when they are desperate for love."

Alex frowned. "Her behavior drove her husband, my stepdad, away. Surely, she would see that and stop. Wouldn't she?"

"I don't know," Pauline said. "It's just a possibility to consider. Now, tell me the story while I try and take a photo of this wombat, who isn't much like I imagined he'd be."

"The story starts at the end of World War Two," Alex said, and began, "This is how my mother told it."

3

25 NOVEMBER 1944

"My mother, Adie, hurried around the corner of the old stone wall, eager to be back at Cheney House where Jocelyn was to introduce her to his parents as his wife. They'd secretly married on his last leave. She almost ran into the policeman who was trying to keep warm by striding around the half-circle entranceway."

"SORRY, LUV," he said, "you can't go in." He stepped in front of her, barring her path and her view.

Adie tried to see around him, concerned at this interruption so near to the end of her journey, but sure it didn't apply to her. She was family and she would be acknowledged as such when Jocelyn got some time away from bombing Germany. And the little one, who made her queasy each morning, was definitely 'family'. She grinned at the thought.

"What's up?" she asked.

"Bombed out," the policeman said, "surprised you didn't hear about it."

He obviously thought she was a village girl who worked at the 'house' and she wanted to put him right, only she had to keep on his good side to find out where Jocelyn's Mum and Dad were. If Jocelyn wasn't here yet, he'd want her to look after them, particularly if they were badly injured. He'd want her to visit the hospital, and when he was back at his base, keep him informed, even look after their affairs if they couldn't.

"Where have the family gone?" she asked.

"They were good people, looked after the poor and that, though I don't personally hold with helping unmarried women who get themselves pregnant, so they've probably gone to a good place," the policeman said with ponderous humor.

"Are they dead?"

"Aye, though there's fewer bodies than were supposed to be in the house. Some of them are just gone, blown to bits."

Adie considered this. She'd only recently met Jocelyn's parents and she knew they didn't approve of her, hence the secrecy, so she couldn't altogether understand her own feelings. Her heart hurt and tears pricked her eyes; her baby would never know its grandparents was the thought that boomed in her head. The policeman hadn't mentioned Jocelyn, so he obviously hadn't arrived home yet, thank God.

"Why would anyone drop bombs here?" she wondered aloud. "It's not like there's anything worth bombing."

"Maybe one of them sluts who couldn't keep her legs together was just as careless about keeping the blackout curtains together," the man replied, "or maybe Jerry just didn't want to get into all the flak over Liverpool, dropped his load early and ran for it."

Adie glared at him, angry at his sneering description of the unmarried mothers Sir Thomas and Lady Maud cared for. She was glad she wasn't showing yet or the man would have thought she was one of them. You'd have thought having some poor soldier's baby would have been a public service, something to be proud of when the men were fighting for freedom and likely to be killed without ever having had the chance for a proper family, but no, everyone sneered and ostracized the girls. Thank God she had Jocelyn. She shivered. Without his love and support, she'd be another unwed mother on her way to a home full of desperate teenage failures.

"Where have they taken the bodies?"

"Graves Brothers, on the High Street," the policeman said. "Actually, if you can identify any of them, we need you to do that. My sergeant lives in the police house just past their place. Call in if you can help."

Adie nodded. "I will," she said, a little frightened by what she might have to view but steeling herself, knowing that the war had finally called on her to play an important part and determined not to shirk it. Jocelyn had to face far worse than this every dark, clear night. "But I didn't really know anyone other than Sir Thomas and Lady Maud."

It was worse than she thought, and when she and the officer returned to the police house, she was grateful for the sergeant's offer of hot sweet tea. Drinking it, unfortunately, made her nausea worse. She fought to keep command of her stomach and won sufficiently well to take notice and plan.

"Can I call my fiancé from here?" she asked, keeping to the cover story of her relationship with Jocelyn. "He should be told about his parents."

"I'm sure the authorities will be getting in touch with him," the sergeant said.

"It will be better from someone he knows," Adie replied, wanting to add 'and loves' but her courage failed her at saying those highly charged words in such a setting. "He'll also want to know I'm alive."

The sergeant led her to his office and handed her the phone. He didn't leave the room – official phones were for official business and it was his job to see that's what it was used for.

Adie dialed the base's number and heard it ringing far away in Yorkshire. The usual man who answered the phone said, "Driffield."

"Can I speak to Squadron Leader Jocelyn de Cheney, please? It's Adie."

"I'm sorry," the man said, his normally friendly tone seemed colder today, "Squadron Leader de Cheney isn't here at the moment. Can I take a message?"

"Has he gone home?" Adie asked. "That's what I'm phoning about. Was he told about his home being bombed?"

"We did get that message but Squadron Leader de Cheney..." the man stopped, then said, "Look, I shouldn't tell you this because you're not really a relative but since Joss introduced us only a week ago, I will. Joss has been missing-in-action since the night before last."

The nausea Adie had been fighting returned. She dropped the phone and fled back into the kitchen to retch in the sink. Dimly, she heard the sergeant speaking to the air base man. She couldn't even remember his name she'd met so many people when she'd been with Jocelyn, and then he put down the receiver. Adie turned on the cold tap to flush away the mess, rinse her face, and hide her tears.

"I'm sorry to be such a nuisance," Adie said as brightly as she could, when the Sergeant joined her in the kitchen. She tidied the sink and dried her hands. She couldn't stop the tears and didn't try.

"Don't worry about it, Miss," the Sergeant said gently, "you've had a nasty shock. You'd best lie down for a while, then we can decide what's to be done."

"I don't need to lie down," Adie said, "and I know what I'm going to do. I'm going to Driffield and I'm going to wait for news about Jocelyn. They'll hear first, now his mum and dad are dead."

"You can't go there," the sergeant said. "They won't let you stay on the base."

"Then I'll sit outside the gates until they get word," Adie said.

ALEX PAUSED, before continuing, "And that's what she did until the commander promised to phone her when they heard what had happened to Jocelyn, even though she wasn't really 'family'. She wanted to explain she was, but as she didn't have the marriage certificate, she thought it best not to argue.

"Word of Jocelyn never came. It was as if he'd just disappeared. Adie questioned others in the squadron and pieced together the last few minutes of 'A for Adie', the name he'd given his Lancaster for good luck. The mental picture of his plane, one wing on fire, sliding out of the sky until it was lost in the smoke billowing from the burning city filled her mind with dread, day and night. She couldn't sleep or eat. She couldn't return to work until she knew – but she never knew."

Pauline shivered. Alex may have been angry with her mother, but the pain wrapped up in the story came through in her words and body language. "The war has a lot to answer for," she said.

Alex nodded. Then she rallied and continued, "She continued hoping until the war ended. Jocelyn wasn't among the posted lists of the liberated prisoners-of-war. She would always say, 'With an aching heart, I packed him away with my other wartime memories.' Her bulging belly, however, couldn't be packed and she was a soon-to-be-single mother in a worn-out, shattered country with a half a million too few men for the women left behind. Then, before she'd even saved enough for the journey to the small country church where she and Jocelyn had married, she met George Wade, an Australian who was handsome, rich, and desperately in love, even though she was carrying someone else's child."

"And they returned home to Wadeville?" Pauline asked.

Alex nodded. "They did," she said.

"And your mother didn't follow up for a copy of her marriage certificate?"

"She said it didn't seem right at the time," Alex said. "I suspect the reason she didn't is because the wedding never happened."

"Maybe she thought she would one day, but life just got in the way."

"Maybe," Alex said. "And maybe, knowing that Cheney Hall was gone, she thought it no longer worth her while to fight for."

4

PAULINE DECIDES TO HELP

"Still, life was looking up if Adie married George Wade," Pauline said.

"Yes," Alex said, "she thought so. They married in London and, when he was demobilized, which was soon after, they came back to live in Wadeville."

Pauline was puzzled. "Alex," she said, "you said Adie believed your stepfather, George Wade, was rich but earlier you said you and your mother were poor. Wasn't he rich, after all?"

"Another sad story, I'm afraid," Alex said. "Mum's luck was dreadful. When she met George Wade, he told her about how the Wades owned all the land around the town of Wadeville, how the town was named after them, and a lot more, they had mines and shares and a huge farm, even by local standards."

"He was from the poor branch of the family?" Pauline guessed.

"Not at all," Alex said, "the bit about him being the heir was perfectly true. Unfortunately, or maybe he didn't know, all the rest was no longer true."

"The Depression had wiped out their shares, the mines had never come to anything, and his dad gambled and lost frequently. He'd mortgaged the property to cover his debts. Much of it had been sold off by the time George and his new English wife got home and the family couldn't afford most of the decencies in life anymore, like servants or hired hands for the farm. George and Mum had to do real farm work just to get by."

"That still doesn't explain why you're poor," Pauline said, "even a farm you have to work yourself is worth serious money when you sell it."

"Mum said my step-granddad was also a drinker," Alex said. "He was killed soon after they arrived back at the farm. A tractor he was driving rolled over and crushed him to death, and by then he'd lost most of the farm, mortgaged the rest and even the insurance company refused to pay the full value of his life insurance because he was drunk when he crashed."

"That doesn't sound too good," Pauline agreed. "But still, your stepfather and your mother could work the farm and get by, couldn't they?"

"They tried," Alex said, "but that was when Dad took to drinking, so Mum said, and she kicked him out."

Pauline said, "But it was his farm, wasn't it?"

Alex nodded. "Yes, but Mum's lawyer got her the farm as her divorce settlement. Unfortunately, there was a drought, and the property wasn't worth much by then. Creditors piled in and by the end we didn't own much anymore. Mum said we were lucky to get out not owing anyone anything."

Again, Alex's gaze focused on eternity and Pauline could only wonder at the awful memories that were running through her mind. Pauline felt she had to help because Adie's story seemed a bit like her own. Pauline hadn't had two unlucky young men in her past, but a war had stolen her happiness with Stephen, just when it seemed to be in reach. Pauline decided, despite her misgivings about Alex's up-and-down temperament, that when she got home, she'd do some investigating on Alex's behalf. It wouldn't make Alex an heiress, she was sure of that, but it may ease the woman's unhappiness.

Alex said, "Dad left us when I was very young. I hardly remember him. I had no idea that he was still alive, to be honest. Until, suddenly, about a week after Mum's funeral, I got a letter from him. He'd seen the notice of mother's death in the paper. It was just a formal letter of condolence, but it included an invitation to visit him if I wanted. For a day or so, I put the letter aside. It seemed like treachery to Mum to acknowledge the man who'd abandoned us both to years of poverty and loneliness. But I have no brothers or sisters, no aunts or uncles, no other relation I know of and I needed to get away from Wadeville." She laughed, a sarcastic, self-mocking sound. "I thought I'd visit him and give him a piece of my mind."

"I can understand that," Pauline said. "I'd feel the same way."

Alex's expression hardened again. Her anger creeping back to the surface. "Except, even in this, mother's stories were twisted," she said.

Pauline knew Alex wasn't angry with her but when someone has this much emotion pent up inside, who knew how it would be vented? "Your visit wasn't what you'd expected?"

"All through the flight from Melbourne to Sydney," Alex said, "I concocted long angry speeches telling him what I thought of him, while I was also wondering what he'd be like. Would he be broken down by drink and poverty, like

Mum had insisted? I imagined him gaunt, frail, and ill like the older drinkers in Wadeville. Should I make it my duty to stand by him in his declining years as I had with Mum through her final illness? Would he even show up at the airport as promised or would he be lying in a gutter somewhere sleeping off another night of debauchery?"

"I assume he wasn't?" Pauline said.

Alex shook her head. "It was nothing like I'd imagined. He's a perfectly ordinary middle-aged man, upright and well-dressed. When he introduced himself as my stepfather, I couldn't believe it. When he introduced his wife, a pleasant, happy woman and his son, I almost wept. The mental picture I'd had of him, born of years of poisonous words, was a sham. Where was the man who spent the farm's profits on drink, rolling home reeking of beer at all hours of the night my mother had told me about?"

"How did he explain the difference?" Pauline asked.

"Very easily," Alex said. "Mother never thought him good enough for her, because she was an aristocrat, and once things began to get difficult, her resentment grew worse. Nothing he did was right. If he went out in the evening for a drink with the other men, she'd accuse him of drunkenness or infidelity."

"Do you remember any of this?" Pauline asked.

"No," Alex said, "except mother was always unhappy. I remember that. I guess that's why Dad wanted to go out to the pub with his mates. I can see that would make mother even more unhappy. I don't remember fights or anything. They probably saved that for when I was at school."

"Meeting your stepfather helped you see a different angle on your life then," Pauline said.

"It did," Alex said, "and though I'd have liked to defend mother, I felt what I was hearing was true. Mum's obsession with us being aristocracy had made both our lives miserable. Maybe Dad wasn't wholly innocent, he was probably much the same as other men, but he wasn't the monster I'd grown up to believe he was. When he told me all this, I suddenly felt sad for mother. I should have been angry with her, twisting both our lives the way she had. You see, in that moment, I felt her disappointment with life so keenly, her bitterness at life's betrayal, her cruel fate; it made me want to cry. I wondered if pain could be passed through a person's genes. At that moment, I felt it could. There I was, in a sunny garden in Sydney blinking back tears for a lost love in a doomed bomber half a world and a lifetime away. It was then I decided that I'd go to England and find out the end of mother's story. It couldn't help her, but it may help me if I put the past to rest."

"What about you and your mother after your stepfather left?" Pauline asked, returning to the earlier part of the story. "Did you stay on the farm?"

Alex shook her head. "For a short while but she couldn't make a go of it. No one would work for her, you see. Her sharp tongue kept them away. Anyway, according to mother, 'the creditors arrived, and we got out with only the shirts on our backs'. We rented a small house in town, which is where I still live today."

"Your mother can't have been very old when she died," Pauline said.

"Life's very unfair you know," Alex said, "and her life more than most, I think. She never smoked or drank, we ate only food from our own garden, or the local store, all the things they tell you to do, and yet she got cancer."

"It must be very hard for you," Pauline said, "when you were so close, only having each other, I mean."

Alex looked at Pauline suspiciously, trying to decide if

Pauline was serious. Then, when she was confident Pauline wasn't being sarcastic, she continued, "We weren't close. I hated her for her idiotic delusions of grandeur." She paused, and then added, "But now, I wish we had been closer."

"You shouldn't be so hard on your Mum, you know," Pauline said. "She did what girls were supposed to do then, marry well and encourage their daughters to go for the best. If fate had been kinder, I'm sure she would have been too."

"You don't really believe me, do you?" Alex said, anger flaring up. "Everything I've said, you're putting down to adolescent rebelliousness or something."

"Of course, I believe you," Pauline said. Alex was going on an angry outburst again and Pauline needed to stop that. "I was just saying you lived so closely with your mother you may have been too close to see the big picture."

"I wish I'd had more time with Mum, now that I know more," Alex agreed. "She was really sick right up to the end, but it made her more pleasant. I guess it gave her a bigger issue to deal with. That's not the way it's supposed to be, is it? Sick people being less snarly I mean. I've missed her so much these past few weeks."

"I can imagine," Pauline said. "I think it wonderful you've made peace with her at the end, even after finding she wasn't entirely honest about your stepfather. I think it says a lot about your character."

"This is going to sound terrible," Alex said, "but I want to tell someone. There were lots of times when I was growing up, I wished my mother was dead. Her behavior to everyone in town and on the farm drove people away from us. We would go weeks without seeing a soul. Even lately when she was sick, I kept thinking what a release it would be for both of us."

"I think we all find our parents embarrassing when we're

growing up," Pauline said, "and when we see them in pain we probably do think dying would be for the best. You shouldn't beat yourself up over it."

Alex nodded but Pauline could see her sympathy wasn't helping and, to be fair, she really had no idea what Alex had gone through. Pauline's parents were nice people, living nice lives, wanting the best for their children, while enjoying the company of neighbors and friends in the place they lived.

After a moment, Alex continued, "Despite all the unkindness that came from my Mother's foolish pride, Mum was my only friend. And, it turned out, I was Mum's only friend too; no one attended her funeral."

That comment gave Pauline a pang of fear. There were occasions now in her own lonely hours that she saw herself being laid to rest without a well-wisher to be found.

"And now?" Pauline asked.

"My trip here and meeting my stepdad has made me think," Alex said. "I don't have to sit at home alone and wither away. If Dad could go from being what her mother called 'a work-shy lay-about who drank the farm's profits' to being a regular family man, then I can stop being an anti-social recluse and become someone who goes abroad and takes part in life."

"Good for you," Pauline said brightly. Though, with her last afternoon running out of time, she was wondering how she was going to finish with this strange encounter. She'd need Alex's address to send anything she learned in Ashton de Cheney to her. Beyond that there didn't seem to be a case for the redoubtable Miss Riddell.

"How will this new life begin?" Pauline asked.

"I'm a legal secretary," Alex said, "so I have savings and I work with documents all the time. What I thought was I'd visit England for a month's vacation and be a sort of detective searching for the truth."

"I'd been thinking of doing some local research for you," Pauline said. "I imagine a country lawyer's work revolves quite heavily around wills so maybe you don't need my help."

"We're not so much into wills in our legal office," Alex replied, "more land sales and transfers, that sort of thing. We did recently have a squabble about a will and a case over some contested land but that's the nearest I've come to anything like this."

"Still, with a background in legal affairs, you should do well searching for what you need," Pauline said. They were almost back at the zoo entrance and the time had come to close this off.

Alex shook her head. "I'd like any help you can give," she said, "particularly on the places before I get there and pointing me in the right direction for documents and such. You see, I only work in the law firm because Mum said it was the one suitable place in town for me to work. It isn't something I have a passion for. I don't have the patience. Mother hoped I'd marry the old lawyer's son, but he chose an outsider, someone he'd met when he was at law school and I'm sort of just there, part of the office furniture."

Pauline, seeing Alex's expression settling into the faraway look she was learning to dread because it meant she'd never escape, said, "Well, if you give me your home address, I'll send you anything I discover." She smiled in what she hoped was a suitable expression for parting.

"Are you taking the ferry?" Alex asked, scrabbling in her bag for paper and pen.

"Yes," Pauline said. "Are you?"

"I'll come with you then," Alex said, "maybe by then I'll find something to write with."

Pauline sighed; she hated disorganization of any kind. She opened her bag, extracted a notebook and pencil, and handed it to Alex.

While Alex wrote her address, Pauline asked, "Are you returning to Wadeville right away or staying on to see some of the wonderful country around Sydney?"

"I've decided to take a tour of the Blue Mountains and visit some opal fields," Alex said, as she returned Pauline's notebook. "I might take up fossicking for opals to make my fortune when I return from England."

"I visited two opal fields last week," Pauline said. "I imagine it's a hard life."

"I've met someone who makes a good living out of finding opals," Alex said, a little defensively. "One of our clients. He said it was an adventurous, uncomplicated way of making money."

"Are you interested in gemstones?" Pauline asked, judging this conversation to be relatively safe. If Alex was interested, it didn't show on her person. Apart from a heavy gold ring on her middle finger, which she fiddled with continuously and was probably her Mother's wedding band, she wasn't wearing a single piece of jewelry.

"I am more interested in finding and selling them," Alex said.

"Australia is a spectacular country," Pauline said, as she sat down on the ferry's outside seats. "Things like regular people just mining precious stones are unheard of where I come from."

"I've never been anywhere else so Australia's just home, I guess. What's England like? Your part I mean?"

Pauline described her present home in Lancashire, and

the nearby Lake District, and Alex nodded. Perhaps, she was comparing notes to her mother's description, Pauline thought.

"It sounds nice," Alex said, when Pauline finished. "I'm looking forward to visiting and seeing places I've heard so much about."

Though she made sure her expression didn't show it, Pauline's heart sank. The polite thing to say, what folks always said in these circumstances, was 'drop by' or 'stay with me' or something like that and she had no over-whelming desire to see Alex again.

"Well, if you do," Pauline said slowly, "get in touch. I'll be happy to help you find places."

"Thank you," Alex replied, "I will if you don't mind. I don't know anyone there and someone to point me in the right direction would be a godsend. You're flying back to England tomorrow?"

"I am," Pauline answered. Then continued, grimacing, "at nine in the morning. I have to be at the airport at some ungodly hour. When do you go back to Wadeville?"

"Next Saturday," Alex said. "I'm staying at my dad's for a few days and doing some sightseeing."

"The opal fields to make your fortune, for example." Pauline said, smiling. "Don't you have *any* money from the farm, now your mother is gone?"

Alex shook her head. "No," she said, "though I am the heir to what's left of the Wade family fortune, which is nothing."

"Your mother must have been quite a catch," Pauline said, smiling. "To marry two rich men."

"I think," Alex said, "she was a scheming gold-digging so-and-so, to be honest."

"It could be just good fortune," Pauline protested.

"Apart from rich people's daughters," Alex replied sarcastically, "how many regular girls meet one heir, let alone two?"

"It does seem a mite suspicious," Pauline agreed. "Well, if there's nothing left of the Wade fortune, I'll see what I can learn about the de Cheney fortune when I get home."

"Thank, you," Alex said. "But don't waste too much of your time on it. I mean to come over and chase it down myself. They are my family, after all, if Mother is to be believed. I haven't taken vacations for years and I have nothing else to do with my time."

"You might want to hear what I discover before you finally decide," Pauline said.

"Oh, it isn't just the money," Alex replied. "I want to research my roots. Mum always made out we were such aristocrats, the two of us. We had to talk properly, dress properly, walk properly, and all the rest of it."

The sadness in Alex's voice tugged at Pauline's heart in the way few other stories ever had, even ones with worse outcomes. She would do her best for Alex and the now dead, Adie, whatever it took, short of having Alex to stay. It would be like living on a volcano. Adie's foolish dreams may not have been a murder or even a crime, but it had done for Alex's life as surely as if it had been. Pauline foresaw a lonely spinsterhood in front of the young woman that was not of her choosing nor of her wish.

They walked off the ferry and headed toward The Rocks, walking slowly, hardly seeing the busy streets around them.

"What was that place where would I find out about my mum and the de Cheney's wills and marriages?" Alex asked, breaking into the silence.

Pauline said, "Somerset House in London has all the

birth registers and marriage certificates going back more than a century. That's all you need really."

"So, if I fly to London," Alex asked, "I can get everything I need there?"

"As far as the paperwork goes, yes."

"How would I get to Lancashire after that?" Alex said.

Pauline told her where to get on the train and where to get off in Manchester, if she chose to stay there, and then added, "Or, if you would like to be closer, get off the train at Preston."

"I'll do that, I think," Alex said, and then added, "You can suggest hotels, I'm sure."

This was the moment Pauline had been hoping to avoid. "Nearer the time, we can organize that," she said.

"Thanks. Will you do me one more favor when you get home?"

"If I can," Pauline said.

"If you find there is such a place as Ashton de Cheney, could you find my grandparents graves, or something like that, and send me a photo? I'd like to have something real as soon as possible. I don't think I can wait now I've begun."

"I'll do my best," said Pauline. "Now this is where I'm staying so I must leave you here." She smiled and held out her hand, "Goodbye for now. I'll send you something very soon, I promise."

Alex shook her hand and walked away toward the train station at Circular Quay.

Pauline watched until she was out of sight then headed back to her room to pack, followed by an early night.

Though she was sorry her trip was over, she packed with a renewed sense of excitement. Her thoughts were all around how quickly she could get started on searching for Ashton de Cheney, which puzzled her immensely. How could she have lived in the district for months and never even heard of the place? Was she always so blind to her surroundings? She'd been busy, it was true, settling into her new house and job, and then the work trips but still, it was odd.

She'd promised Alex she wouldn't research the actual people; that was Alex's search. She would look only for places or things and scout the territory for Alex's arrival. Nevertheless, Pauline thought she'd know the truth of Alex's mother's story long before Alex arrived.

5

SURPRISES EVERYWHERE

P ushing open the front door, half expecting to find it stuck with a pile of junk mail like on a TV comedy, Pauline entered her house. But her neighbor had been as good as her word. The mail, including all the flyers and handouts, was stacked neatly on the hall table. She carried her cases inside and closed the door. This was when the cloistered life failed to appeal. The house was silent and cold, musty smelling and not at all welcoming.

For an hour Pauline bustled about, making tea, turning up the heating, unpacking, enjoying the activity after being cooped up in planes and taxis for a day. She walked down to the village store and bought the usual supplies, before making a small, simple meal. She hardly knew what to call the meal for her body's internal clock was all askew.

When the daylight faded, and the lights were on, she finally listened to the messages on her newly installed telephone answering machine. Its red lamp had been flashing accusingly at her throughout the afternoon. She discovered her boss was not pleased, but she hadn't expected he would be, so she skipped past those, and she learned her mum wanted her to visit the farm for a family birthday, which was next weekend. Pauline couldn't help feeling she'd be working because her boss was so incensed and likely to demand her time. She'd call them both back tomorrow when she was feeling stronger.

The following day was Sunday, so after church, she called her boss who she knew wouldn't be in church, unless the devil was now doing divine services too. He was home. He would have been on the golf course, but the weather was bad. A howling gale and driving rain weren't good for golf.

If Pauline had imagined this inability to golf would make her boss's temper even worse, she was pleasantly surprised to find it hadn't. The 'emergency' that had been preying on his mind when he'd left the messages had been dealt with by her colleagues and everything was sweetness and light again in the office. He didn't actually say don't rush back but it was close enough for Pauline to confidently call her mother and agree to attend the birthday party on the following weekend.

"Well, I should think so," her mother said when Pauline had agreed to come. "It's your sister's birthday and you should be here."

"I have a job that doesn't always leave weekends free, Mum," Pauline said, "a bit like yours and Dad's."

"Nonsense," her mother said. "We have animals that have to be tended to, not papers to sort. They can be done anytime."

Knowing this discussion could go on forever, as it often felt to Pauline, she calmly replied, "Well, I'll be there. What would Freda like for a present?"

The conversation, diverted onto uncontroversial topics,

flowed better and Pauline let her mother talk while she considered her own next steps. The Whalley Church and Library would be good places to start. The library would have local village history books and documents, while the church would have the parish register, and the graveyard where the de Cheneys would likely be buried. The librarians and the vicar would also likely know people who were researching local history. Some of those people could tell her all she needed to know; she was sure.

After work the next day, Pauline headed straight to the church and library. She was right. Both had information to impart, though perhaps not as much as she'd hoped for.

"I'm afraid I can't personally be of much service," the vicar of St. Mary's and All Saints said when Pauline met him at the church door. "I've only been here about a year and I'm not even a local."

Pauline wasn't surprised at his words. With his curly red hair and pale freckled face, the vicar looked about seventeen but was presumably older than that.

"The parish registry will have the information I want," Pauline said.

"And the church itself," the vicar replied. "There are plaques and pews commemorating the de Cheneys as far back as the 1600s."

"May I take photos?"

"Certainly," said the vicar, "but this isn't the church you want. The old de Cheney church is a mile away on the Clitheroe road."

"Is there a vicar there?" Pauline asked, hopeful of an older, more knowledgeable incumbent.

"I'm the vicar there too," he said. "The parishes were merged many years ago. Few people attend church nowadays."

"Will it be open if I drive up there now?" Pauline asked.

"I'm going there as it happens. Follow me and I'll let you in."

Pauline followed the vicar's ancient Morris Minor through the darkness. He stopped at an old building, backlit by the lights of houses behind a thin screen of trees.

"Here we are," the vicar said, unlocking the large wooden doors with an old-fashioned key. "Australia, you said. The descendant lives in Australia?"

"Yes," Pauline said shortly, anxious to get on with her work.

"The ladies of the local historical society would be interested to hear from her," the vicar continued. "They're always looking out for stories of old Ashton de Cheney. There's so little left now."

"I'll ask Alex when I speak to her next," Pauline said, edging past the vicar and into the dimly lit church. The winter sun barely penetrated the old stained glass. The vicar followed Pauline inside and turned the lights on.

"This old church was made for brighter days than these heathen times," the vicar said with a sad smile.

Pauline looked about. Apart from the windows, the church was simply furnished, more 'Low' than 'High' Anglican. Perhaps the de Cheney family had moved from Catholic to a simpler form of worship through the centuries. It wasn't unusual in older families.

"The de Cheney pews were over there," the vicar said. "They had their own door too, at that side of the church. A path led straight from the door to their house. You can see where it ran if you go around to that side."

"Thank you, vicar," Pauline said with finality. She really wanted to look about on her own.

"I have some items to collect in the vestry," the vicar

replied. "If I'm not out when you're ready to leave, be sure to pull the door closed when you go."

Pauline scanned the plaques on the wall, noting the dates, following the family through the centuries. It was a conventional enough record: elder son followed elder son as Baronet, while younger brothers joined the Army and Navy where they died, some violently, most not, without particular distinction.

Finally, he found Sir Thomas and Lady Maud on a simple plaque, as befitted post-wartime austerity, placed by 'friends and neighbours'. The poignancy of the plain words, commemorating the end of centuries of de Cheney life, affected Pauline more than anything she'd ever researched before. She did her best with the camera but even with the church lights on, she couldn't be sure the photo would be any good.

"I'm glad they were well enough liked," she said quietly to no one in particular, "for the village to want to remember them." Somehow the knowledge made her inquiries even better.

Pauline took notes, called goodbye and thanks through the vestry door, and as requested, pulled the church door closed behind her. As a churchgoer she believed churches should always be open but, sadly, nowadays churches were no safer than they had been in Viking times. That was the extent of modern progress; society had returned to the ninth century.

In the graveyard, she found the small mausoleum the vicar had given her directions to and took its photo as well. Again, the simple plaque commemorating Sir Thomas and Lady Maud was heartbreaking in its simplicity. It did have one further embellishment, however, 'and their son, Sir

Jocelyn de Cheney.' It seemed, sometime later, the missing airman had been counted among the dead.

Pauline hurried back to the village and the library, hoping to catch the staff before they started closing.

The staff was one elderly lady who looked like she'd read every book the library stocked.

"We don't have a lot of information on the old village," she said, when Pauline told her she was looking for books on Ashton de Cheney. "What we have is through here." She led Pauline into a smaller room where non-fiction books were kept. "Most people go to Manchester for historical research," she continued, "even the schoolchildren. We mainly just do novels nowadays." Her tone of voice said she wasn't happy about that. "And I know a lot about the village if you can't find what you need."

"Are you from this area?" Pauline asked.

"Not really, not from old Ashton, not even from Whalley," she replied. "My husband and I came here in the Sixties."

Pauline thanked her for her help and selected the local newspaper file from the shelf. She flicked through the pages and was immediately rewarded by articles about the bombing in 1944.

Pauline read the articles with a sinking heart. She photocopied them before going back to see the librarian.

"Did you find what you wanted?" she asked when she saw Pauline approach.

"Enough for today," Pauline said as cheerfully as she could. "I wondered. The vicar mentioned an historical society. Are you a member?"

"Certainly, I am," she replied. "Ashton de Cheney in the Stuart period is my forte. Why do you ask?"

I would have guessed prim Victorian, Pauline thought smiling inwardly. She didn't look the swashbuckling Cavalier or grim Puritan type.

"I wondered if any of the Society was familiar with the events of November 25, 1944."

"Well, we all are, of course. It was a sad day for the village. In a way that was the day the village died, though it wasn't until after the war it disappeared into Whalley."

Pauline explained her interest but restrained herself from asking if there was any mention of an Adelaide Fuller in the Historical Society records as a wife or fiancée to Jocelyn. Her promise to Alex, only to research the locations, forbade her going further.

"The vicar suggested Alex and the Society should meet, could you arrange that?"

"I'd be delighted. I'm Celia Ormiston by the way," the librarian said, holding out her hand. "I'm always here; drop by when you know the dates your Australian friend will be in town. We have some other records your friend might find interesting. Let me show you."

Pauline followed Celia to the small room at the back of the library where the few remaining records were kept.

"I think you'll find more than you need here," Celia said, as she left Pauline to look through the titles. "Even though it is a very small selection, it covers the whole period of the region's history."

"This may sound like a silly question but where is Ashton de Cheney today?" Pauline asked.

"Sadly, it remains only in names of parks and streets," Celia said. "It was swallowed up by the surrounding towns in the rebuilding after the war. You'll find a map in the book, *Old Ashton*, on the higher shelf over there." She pointed to

Pauline's right, where a coffee table sized book protruded beyond the shelf.

Pauline thanked her and began her search, which lasted until the library closed.

"Did you find all you needed?" Celia asked as Pauline left.

"I think I did, thank you," Pauline said. "I will probably be back over the next weeks, if Alex asks to know more."

"The library is always here," Celia said, "but why not join us on Tuesday night at the next meeting of the Historical Society? I'm sure a lot of questions could be answered more fully there. We have members who know everything about their own preferred period and those last days are one of the most popular periods. Everyone has an opinion about that."

"Thank you," Pauline said. "I will." She took down the details of time and place of the meetings and headed out into the night, where a stiff breeze was blowing sleety rain down the length of the street. She hardly noticed the rain for her mind was entirely engaged in trying to decide what to tell Alex. The vicar's and librarian's advice had proved to be devastatingly accurate. The local library's archives provided all she needed. The trouble was, it ended Alex's quest before it had really begun.

At home, she made a hot cup of tea to drive out the chill that seemed to have invaded the very marrow of her bones and re-read the photocopy of the local newspaper dated 26 November 1944.

'Death of Lord and Lady de Cheney

Sir Thomas and Lady Maud de Cheney were killed instantly by two bombs that hit their family home, Cheney House, during Saturday night's raid on Liverpool. Their deaths are made more poignant by the news that their only son, and heir to the estate,

Squadron Leader Jocelyn de Cheney, has been missing in action since Thursday night.

Lord and Lady de Cheney's charitable work among the poor of Manchester and their recent opening of Cheney House to destitute unmarried mothers will be remembered for as long as people of goodwill survive...'

Or at least until they're buried, Pauline thought sarcastically. Then she remembered the plaque and felt slightly ashamed by her cynicism.

'A complete list of the unfortunate girls killed in the tragedy is not yet available to this correspondent, but one guest at least survived. Miss Adelaide Fuller was away from the house visiting friends that night...'

Pauline stopped reading. Was any other interpretation possible? Did the word 'guest' suggest Adelaide was something other than an unmarried mother-to-be? She thought it could not. Now how was she to tell Alex without breaking her heart? Pauline thought that Alex was reconciled to not inheriting a great estate but how easily would she take learning she almost certainly wasn't even related to the de Cheneys? Pauline decided to think very carefully about the letter that she'd have to write.

Fortunately, until she had the film processed and knew if the photos she'd taken of the plaques and mausoleum were legible, she had nothing to write about so she could take care in crafting a letter that, she hoped, would let Alex down gently.

However, the chemist shop where she'd left the film for processing was pleasantly quick with her prints and they were clear enough for Alex to see their content. So, only two days later, Pauline placed them in an air mail envelope with her already written letter and sent it off to Alex. She shouldn't expect a return letter for a week or two and that was just fine in her mind. She had real work to do in the world of accounting. The de Cheney inheritance mystery was done and dusted.

6

PAULINE IS FIRED

A little over a week later, as Pauline was poring over a folder of papers she'd brought home from her latest work assignment, her phone rang.

"Hello," she said absently, her focus still very much on the tables of figures before her.

"I thought you were on my side," Alex yelled accusingly in her ear.

Stunned by this outburst, Pauline said, "I am."

"You were supposed to be helping, not finding reasons to stop," Alexandra interrupted her angrily.

"Alex, listen—"

"No. You listen," Alex shouted. "You promised not to touch the people. They're mine, not yours. You thought you'd show me what a clever little researcher you are, didn't you? Well, you can forget it. I'll do it myself. Goodbye!"

The phone slammed down, leaving Pauline bemused. She couldn't call back because while she'd given Alex her phone number, Alex hadn't given Pauline hers. For a moment, Pauline felt angry. Then her professional detachment asserted itself. She'd heard a lot worse from incompetent and criminal accountancy workers these past years; it was all just water off a duck's back. She felt sorry for Alex but at least she wouldn't now descend on Pauline's quiet private life and disturb it. And, if Alex cooled down enough to read the letter again maybe she would see it was for the best.

With something of a wry grin, Pauline thought about how carefully she'd worked on the letter to Alex, trying so hard to soften the woman's disappointment. Clearly, she hadn't quite captured that softening effect. On the other hand, it had confirmed something she'd always found unsettling. Now she could really see why her forensic accounting colleagues insisted on writing the final reports and asked her only to provide the data, analysis, and conclusions. If Alex's response was anything to go by, Pauline just didn't have the knack of saying things the right way. It was a learning moment and one she could live with, or work to improve – sometime.

7

THE HISTORICAL SOCIETY

Celia Ormiston introduced Pauline to the assembled group of generally middle-aged ladies, one bearded, long-haired young man who was an historian at the local college, a scrupulously groomed man sitting outside the group who was, apparently, the Society's lawyer, and an older man who chaired the meeting. With the introductions made, she invited Pauline to tell them what she knew about Alex and her connection to Ashton de Cheney.

Pauline briefly outlined how she'd met Alex and told them the story that Alex had been told by her mother. There was some muttering at the suggestion that Alex's mother had been engaged, or even married, to Jocelyn de Cheney but she was allowed to continue. Finally, Pauline said, "My own brief look into the events of those last days of the de Cheney's suggests her mother may have embellished her role with regard to the family."

"I'd say she did," one of the older women said. "There was never any suggestion of an engagement or marriage between Jocelyn and any woman. I was young when all this happened, of course, but I'm sure it would have been known."

"I've read that newspaper article," another woman said, "and I agree with you, Miss Riddell. This young woman's mother took advantage of the family tragedy to weave a romantic tale for her Australian husband and daughter. Quite a wicked fairy tale, I'd say."

There was a murmur of agreement at this, which Celia Ormiston interrupted by saying, "When we met at the library, Miss Riddell, you said the young woman was planning to visit England and Ashton, is that still the case?"

"At the time we spoke, that was her intention," Pauline replied. 'However, I sent her a letter with photos and the photocopy of the news article, and I've reason to believe she may not visit now."

"Probably for the best," the bearded man said. "She's not to blame for her mother's story but she would be terribly hurt when the truth finally sinks in."

"I fear she already is," Pauline said. "I tried to break the news gently but when you've been taught to believe something from a young age, it's hard to let it go, I imagine."

"Well, from our point of view," Celia said, "as an historical research group, we have gained a snippet of information we didn't have before. Adelaide Fuller, the young woman mentioned in the newspaper article, married and went to Australia. We can add that as a footnote to the story."

"Thank you for inviting me to be here tonight," Pauline said, as there seemed to be no further interest among the members. "If I do hear from Alex again, and she decides to visit after all, I'll let you know."

"Please do," the chairman said. "Celia is easy to find at the library and my business office is on the High Street. I think I'm right in saying we'd all like to learn more about how Adelaide Fuller's story played out. Your friend, Alex, could come to one of our meetings. We'd be happy to hear more."

The assembled group murmured their goodbyes and thanks as Pauline gathered her coat, gloves, and hat before leaving. The chairman nodded dismissal. As she turned to go, her eyes caught the lawyer's and something about his expression rubbed Pauline the wrong way. She never trusted men who were too well-dressed. She left the building, turning her collar up against the dampness, and walked home in a pensive mood. The chairman had said he thought the group would be happy to meet and hear from Alex. Pauline knew she wasn't the most empathetic person in the world, but she felt sure most of the committee would be hostile rather than happy if Alex came to the meeting. And with someone as volatile as Alex, the meeting would end badly. Luckily, that was unlikely to happen now.

The following morning the phone rang. Pauline ambled from the kitchen to answer it, still nibbling on her breakfast of a thin slice of toast and thick cut Dundee marmalade.

"Hello," she said, after making sure no sticky bits of jam were adhering to her mouth and fingers. She couldn't abide sticky phones. One of the best innovations at her place of work was the woman who came in at night and sanitized every phone in their offices.

"I'm sorry about the other day, Pauline" she heard Alex say. "I was just so disappointed when I started reading your letter."

"I'm disappointed too," Pauline said calmly.

"I understand," Alex said. "It was ungracious of me, I know. I can't apologize enough."

"You've read my letter properly now?" Pauline asked.

"Yes, and you say it's not certain that my mother was lying."

"Exactly. Nothing is ever really certain – definitely not in history," Pauline said, "but in this case there's no big picture, no dynastic squabble, no territory to be won or lost, not even a grand de Cheney estate. Most of it had been lost in the Depression, so it's hard to see why the truth shouldn't be as sad as it appears."

"You think she made up the story the moment she realized everyone who knew the truth about her was dead?"

"Yes, I do," Pauline answered. "I thought it best you hear about it before you wasted your life savings on an airline ticket."

"I understand why you don't want me to visit after the way I shouted at you," Alex said, "but I think I might still visit England. I've heard so much about it from Mother and I'd like to see some of the places I heard so much about."

"I have no problem with you visiting," said Pauline. "I just want you to be prepared to enjoy your sightseeing because you aren't likely to hear anything to your advantage. It's unlikely you have a claim on the estate or to the de Cheney family name."

"She couldn't have made it all up," Alex said. "Really, it would be too cruel to make my life, her husband's life, and her own life a misery for a lie."

"Maybe the story was just her way of coping or of keeping you to herself. Maybe she just liked being special and single with an adoring daughter. The story was her way of doing what she wanted to do anyway."

"So, you think there's nothing in all this for me?" asked Alex. "I don't mean money; I mean a family, a place, roots."

"Your mother must have had parents," Pauline replied.

"You may have uncles and aunts, cousins, nephews, and nieces."

"I suppose," Alex said. "It sounds completely deflating."

"And," Pauline said, "as I wrote in my letter, you shouldn't let your hopes be dashed entirely because your search is just beginning. Whenever anyone researches their family history, they always seem to get the bad news first."

"I will book a flight," Alex said, "and let you know as soon as I have the details."

"Good," Pauline said, "and, who knows, by then I may have heard more hopeful news that will make the whole trip worthwhile."

"I never really believed I was an heiress, you know," Alex continued, "but I hoped I might get something from it, a family maybe, or... I don't know what, a heritage, if you like. Now it looks like I'm more orphaned than I was before."

"Is there somewhere I can call you if I hear more?" Pauline asked. "Letters aren't a good way of communicating this stuff."

"Call me here at work," Alex said and gave her the number. "I'm only in the office during the week but there's an answering machine."

Pauline hung up the phone and returned to her breakfast deep in thought. Having a complete stranger in her house was never going to be easy; she'd become too used to her own space, and Alex was the sort of person who flew off the handle at trifles. Pauline had been understanding up to now, but she wasn't the type of person to put up with that forever.

8

THE HEIRESS ARRIVES

When Alex's flight was confirmed, Pauline booked a Friday evening train from Manchester to London and reserved two rooms in a quiet hotel close to Somerset House, Britain's document repository. This was the place where Alex needed to spend some time before traveling north or even think of sightseeing.

With her plans made, the following evening Pauline dropped into the library on her way home from work. She soon found Celia Ormiston.

"I am glad she's decided to visit," Celia said. "I only hope our more censorious Society members don't get carried away by their own rhetoric."

"They do seem likely to do that," Pauline said. "To be honest, I'm going to advise Alex not to attend."

Celia nodded. "They are only too likely to get heated, I'm afraid, because they all have their own pet views on everything. And they're all sentimentally attached to poor Sir Jocelyn. Having someone who claims to be his daughter turn up may be like a red rag to a bull. It may be for the best if your friend doesn't come to a meeting, but I hope she will."

Pauline nodded her agreement. "Perhaps," Pauline said, "Alex could meet with you or a few carefully selected members, those who can be trusted not to attack the witness, if you'll pardon my allusion."

Celia nodded. "That would be a good idea," she said. "I'll put that to the others at the meeting tonight. If they think they'll be excluded, they may promise to be on their best behavior. You say it's this weekend she's arriving?"

"Yes," Pauline replied. "It's short notice, but Alex is very keen to make the trip now she's decided to do it. I'm meeting her at Heathrow on Saturday morning and we're staying near Somerset House so she can spend the first few days of her visit researching as well as sightseeing all that London has to offer."

"The middle of winter when it's dark most of the day isn't the best time to see London or anywhere here," Celia said, grimacing. "It will be quite a shock after the Australian sunshine, I would think."

"I tried to persuade her next spring would be a better time," Pauline agreed, "but she has the bug now so she's arriving Saturday."

"I'll let the group know," Celia said, "and start preparing them to be other than their usual selves."

The journey down to London on Friday night was as cold and uncomfortable as all train trips were nowadays, Pauline thought sourly, as it rattled and clattered over the rails in the darkness. The engine hauling the carriages may no longer be driven by steam, but the carriages were from those earlier days and the wear and tear wasn't being hidden by the superficial fixes applied to keep them operational.

The taxi from the station to the hotel was equally old. The country just wasn't pulling out of the nosedive it had taken during and after the war, or at least not as well as the other countries she visited as part of her work. If her parents died, Pauline thought somberly, there'd be no over-whelming reason to stay here.

By Saturday morning, however, in daylight and after a night's rest, the future looked brighter. She had a guest to show the sights to, a small, unthreatening mystery to help clear up, and a weekend in London. Life wasn't as bad as it sometimes presented itself during the dark hours. By mid-morning, she was in a taxi on her way to Heathrow to meet the flight from Sydney. She'd need to be cheerful when she met Alex because she knew exactly how Alex would be feeling. Her own flights to, and from, Australia had left her washed out for days after.

"Alex," Pauline called, waving at her as she stepped uncertainly through the doors out into Heathrow Airport's arrivals area. Pauline could tell the crowds milling around the corded-off walkway distressed Alex. She looked stunned by the noise.

"Good flight?" Pauline asked, shaking her hand briefly before taking her bags and leading her toward the exit.

"Yes, thanks," Alex answered slowly, "I'm sorry," she added, "my mind is totally jet lagged."

"It's not far to the hotel," Pauline lied, as they waited for the taxi driver to load the bags into the car. "Then I suggest you freshen up and we go out for a while."

"I just want to die," Alex wailed, "or failing that, sleep."

"I know how you feel," said Pauline with a laugh, as the driver closed the door behind them, "but believe me, it's best to get into the time and routine of wherever you are as soon as possible."

"I will, when I know when and where I am," Alex said, smiling sleepily.

"London and it's just past noon," Pauline replied.

While Pauline pointed out the landmarks she recognized, Alex stared silently through the window watching the city slide by. In truth, Pauline thought, it wasn't surprising Alex was dozing for the narration Pauline was giving wasn't very interesting. Mainly because there weren't many landmarks she knew; her visits to the capital had been to the center and more concerned with work than sightseeing.

When they reached the hotel, Alex allowed Pauline to lead her to her room. They'd decided days earlier, by phone, that they'd save money by sharing a room. It was Alex's idea and Pauline understood her wish not to be too big a burden on her hostess, but Pauline found she couldn't face that and had booked two rooms. She needed her space too much for sharing.

When she saw Alex safely inside, Pauline said, "Take your time, but if you're quick, we can use last hours of the afternoon looking in the documents at Somerset House. Even if you just learn your way about that will be a good start. I'm just in the room next door; knock on the door when you're ready."

Seeing Alex's numbed expression, Pauline was sure they wouldn't get any work done today but she was wrong. After only thirty minutes or so, there was a knock on her bedroom door. She opened it.

"I want to go straight to Somerset House," Alex said.

Pauline grinned. "You're doing better than I did when I flew back," she said, and then added, "I was sure I wouldn't see you until morning."

"I sloshed water on my face, changed into clean clothes and now I'm fine," Alex replied. "I can't wait to start."

"Excellent," said Pauline. "We can't do everything today, but we can start. Then maybe a light dinner and an early night?"

"I'm ready to paint the town red, thank you," Alex said. "I have a new lease on life."

"Then follow me," Pauline said, fastening her coat and wrapping her scarf around her neck.

The December afternoon was dry and frosty, which seemed to perk Alex up even more. She seemed practically light-headed by the time they stood outside Somerset House and planned their next move. A thin, cold wind blowing up the Thames from the sea fluttered their clothes, nipping their noses and ears.

Pauline said, "I suggest you start with marriages. That's the heart of it and nothing else will matter if they turn out favorable."

"Exactly right," said Alex. "If I find Mum's marriage certificate to Jocelyn de Cheney I'm practically home and dry."

"Then I'll leave you to it," Pauline said, "unless you desperately need my help?"

"If I don't find what I'm looking for, I'll come and find you and then you can help. But I work with documents all the time, it should be a doddle."

Pauline laughed. "Meet here when the place closes," she said. Alex agreed and strode inside. Pauline turned to survey the river and the embankment. What she needed was a nice cup of tea and a scone.

9

SOMETHING IS WRONG

After her afternoon tea and a Sally Lunn bun, Pauline made her way back to Somerset House as the time for closing drew near, arriving at the entrance at almost the same moment Alex exited the building.

"How was the search?" Pauline asked. "Did you find what you were looking for?"

"No," Alex said shortly. Her expression was hard and angry.

"Perhaps we should head back to the hotel," Pauline said. "It's been a long day for you."

"I'm fine," Alex replied. "In fact, I feel a whole lot better now I'm outside."

Her expression didn't convince Pauline, but she couldn't actually force the woman to rest so she said, "Then we'll walk along the embankment until it's time to eat."

Alex nodded. They walked back toward the heart of the city, jostled by the crowds of people hurrying home, heads down against the wintry night. All around the great city grumbled and roared. The constant vibration from feet and traffic made the earth below their feet seem alive.

At the embankment, Alex stopped and gazed around. "You know, I've seen all this before in pictures and movies," she said. "I never really thought I'd actually be here."

"Does it look as you expected?"

"Yes, it does. It looks like it's been here forever," she said. "Not like home. Home looks like someone put it up that morning and it could be taken down at night. London looks as if it grew right out of the earth." She watched a riverboat cruise by, lit in seasonal colors, and loaded with diners. A reflection of the elegantly lit Houses of Parliament shimmered on the river's surface as the boat's wake broke the picture into a galaxy of glittering points of light.

"Where are we walking to?" Alex asked.

"I booked us into a restaurant near the hotel," Pauline said. "We're just passing the time until our reservation, and your batteries run out."

"You're going to be disappointed there," Alex said. "I feel stronger with every step we take. And the air is so bracing I may never sleep again."

"Good," Pauline said, "then let's keep going."

Alex's dark mood seemed to be lifting with the evening air and the scene before them. Suddenly, she said, "Mum spent her last months in England living in London. It's where she met George Wade."

"Perhaps they walked right here," Pauline replied.

"Perhaps," Alex said, "but in Mum's case I don't believe she felt much joy. I'm not sure I do right now either."

"Two men loved your mum enough to marry her," Pauline said. "She must have been lovable when she was young and lovable usually means loving."

"Men are often misled by their desires, I'm told," Alex

replied with a harsh laugh, "but I know what you mean, and I still think it incredible. I never saw that in her."

"We don't always see our parents as others do, or as they see each other," Pauline said. "Are you sure both men were misled?"

"Both men were aristocratic heirs to large estates," said Alex, "and Mum wasn't born into those circles."

"I see you've been thinking about this a lot since I called and gave you the bad news," Pauline said, "but are you sure it isn't just your own bitterness prejudicing you against her?"

"Possibly," Alex admitted. "On the other hand, you must admit it is unusual for an ordinary girl to have such good fortune twice. Even these days, never mind back then when people didn't mix so much."

"You're forgetting the war," Pauline said, guiding her into the doorway of an Italian restaurant. "That led to a lot of social mixing."

"Maybe," Alex conceded as she stepped inside. After the cold street, the room seemed superheated. They quickly handed their coats to a man while a waiter took them to their seats. The restaurant wasn't full; it was still early for London diners.

"I didn't think Australia had aristocrats," Pauline said, when they'd placed their orders. "I remember being told so. Often."

"I'm sure you know very well everywhere has aristocrats," Alex replied. "They just go by different names. George was heir to the Wade family fortune, as he told Mum, the premier family in Wadeville. The town was named after them." Alex sipped the wine they'd ordered, staring moodily into its dark color.

"You don't need to convince me," Pauline said. "I'm the one who has to bite her tongue every time she sees or hears the media rail against true aristocrats and then listen and watch them fawning over the present crop of robber barons who make our lives a misery."

"That sounds a lot like revolutionary talk," Alex said. "I hope you're not a socialist."

"I'm not," Pauline said, "I just wish people didn't need leaders, but they do. The best you can hope for is that they choose the mildly criminal over the wildly criminal. That's why I like the old aristocracy over new money. The fire's gone out of the old ones and they lead gently if you'll follow."

"Well," said Alex with a tired smile, "when I come into my inheritance, I hope you'll remember you said that."

"Sure," said Pauline, "I'll be as subservient as you please." It seemed like a plan to keep her mood up now she was talking.

Pauline wondered if Alex was going to make it through dinner, she was wilting so fast. "What are the plans for tomorrow?" She spoke loudly to jolt Alex awake.

"Sightseeing," Alex, startled, said, "because my 'quest' as I thought of it is over."

"Weren't you successful in births and marriages?" Pauline asked. Alex's scowl suggested she hadn't been.

"It is as you said," Alex replied. "I found Lord and Lady de Cheney's marriage certificate and Mum's to George Wade but not one for Mum to Jocelyn de Cheney. By the way, the only reason I found the one between Mum and George Wade was because she described herself on the marriage license as Adelaide de Cheney, not Fuller. Cheeky, eh? But it makes me wonder if even that marriage was legal when it wasn't made out in her real name."

That seemed to bring an end to the conversation as it was followed by their meal arriving and they ate in morose silence. Pauline watched Alex's head beginning to nod as the meal wore on and she let the silence do its work. With luck, Alex would finally agree to get some rest.

They left the building, pulling their coats around their ears to keep out the wind that still swept along the Thames, swirling around in London's wet streets, and nipping their extremities. They walked back toward their hotel, along with the seemingly millions of others making their way home at the end of the day.

"Did you get to birth certificates?" Pauline asked, when Alex's gloom was becoming positively creepy.

"Yes. I found Mother's and Jocelyn's," Alex said. "I was born in Australia and have an Australian birth certificate. It shows George Wade as the father. Still, I'd hoped there'd be something to point to a de Cheney connection here."

"More may show up tomorrow when you research the death certificates," Pauline said, a little too heartily.

"I'm not wasting my time or yours on another day chasing a figment of my mother's twisted imagination," Alex said. "Tomorrow we head up to Lancashire. You can show me around and then I'm done."

"Don't be silly," Pauline said. "Finish your research here, it would only take another day."

"I'm not being silly," Alex retorted, "I'm being sensible. There's nothing here for me but Mum's old memories and twisted tales."

Mentally cursing herself for her choice of words, Pauline tried to rectify the situation. "Research takes time," she said. "Trust me, I do a lot of it."

"Oh, you do, do you? How do you know so much about it?" Alex asked.

"My job is forensic accounting. We dig into records all the time and in my—"

"Experience," finished Alex. "But your experience told me this was a hopeless exercise weeks ago, or don't you remember? Which experience should I trust, your first answer or this new advice?"

"It's your vacation and your quest," Pauline said mildly. "I just think, to be sure, you should research the death certificates and wills on Monday."

"We know when they died, for God's sake," Alex cried. "It says so in the paper."

"We don't know when Jocelyn died," Pauline continued stubbornly.

"Well, there won't be a death certificate in Somerset House for him, will there?" Alex was almost screaming with weariness and disappointment. A day of flying, followed by hunting down wrong families and names, coupled with the disappointment of not finding the crucial marriage certificate, seemed to have finished her from historical research forever.

"Not if he died in Germany, no," Pauline admitted.

"So, I'm going to Lancashire," Alex said. "You can show me around or not, please yourself."

"Why not spend tomorrow in London, do some sightseeing, go to the theater," Pauline continued, patiently, "and then travel up the next day."

Alex seemed about to scream 'No!' but stopped in time. "All right," she said when she'd recovered her composure. "I'd like that."

"What places would you like to see?"

Alex considered. "Mum mentioned Buckingham Palace, the Houses of Parliament, and some other things. I'll try and remember. We should go to them, follow her footsteps."

"Okay," Pauline said, "you work on remembering while

you have an early night. The flight over from Oz takes a lot out of you."

"I'm fine," Alex lied. She looked anything but fine.

Pauline didn't say anything more and they walked on together in silence. Wet pavements shone gold, reflecting the overhead sodium lamps, a thin icy rain had begun to fall. It soaked through their coats as they walked, heads down, against the raw December night. The shops were shut and dark. Only pubs spilled welcoming signs of light and merriment out into the street from their open doorways. The noise of rock music echoed hollowly from 'The Bull' at the crossroads just ahead of them.

"England in winter," Alex said, suddenly, "is a cold place."

"It's the damp," said Pauline. "It isn't actually cold; the temperature is well above freezing anyway." She glanced up at the sound of an approaching car, puzzled by something about it. The car swept past the small roundabout at the junction, accelerating as it came. That's what was odd, she realized, it should have been slowing. She stiffened. When it mounted the pavement, Pauline leapt aside, dragging Alex with her. She heard a thump, felt Alex jerk in her grip. They landed heavily on the ground and Pauline rolled them both away from the rear wheel spinning wildly on the slick surface beside her face. The car, engine racing, hurtled back onto the road and down the street. Only when it reached the junction and the end of the streetlamps, did the driver put on its lights.

10

THERE MUST BE SOMETHING

"**A**re you all right?" Pauline asked. They were laying against the wall, below a shop window whose fluorescent security lighting cast a pale glow on Alex's even paler face.

"My leg hurts," she said.

Pauline sat up. Alex's leg was bare almost to her thigh, the tattered pantyhose ripped from her leg hung at her ankle. Blood oozed from an ugly gash below her knee but there were no unnatural angles to her leg – no bones protruding.

"Can you walk?" Pauline asked, looking about for assistance. The street was empty. It was too early for people to come out of the pubs, too late for shoppers, and too wet for idle strollers. She would have to support Alex if she couldn't walk unaided. She couldn't carry her.

"I think so," Alex said. "Nothing feels broken."

Pauline helped her to her feet, and they stood together, composing themselves, while Alex felt for injuries that weren't visible to the eye.

"That was someone who'd been celebrating the season a

bit too well," Alex said with a forced laugh as they limped away, her arm around Pauline's shoulder.

"I think they were trying to kill us," Pauline said, aware it sounded melodramatic.

"Somebody you upset with your forensic auditing you think?"

Pauline shook her head, saying, "That's a good theory but I don't live in London and none of the projects I've worked on were around here. Much of our work is international. It isn't me they were after."

"Well," said Alex, "in case you'd forgotten, I got off a plane about six hours ago and I don't know anyone in the whole country except you. So, it definitely isn't me. Let's face it: it's the holidays; everyone's in the pub drinking; it's dark, foggy and wet, and my explanation is the right one."

"I guess," said Pauline running through the events in her mind again, this time imagining a drunk driver. He – she thought the shadowy outline of the driver was a man – came out from the pub, got in his car and drove onto the main street where the lights were so bright, he didn't notice he'd forgotten to put on his own car lights. Before his befuddled brain had gotten hold of where he was, he was at the junction. Too late to slow or stop, he accelerated to get across before another car came. Maybe he was fiddling with the radio, or a music tape, lost his concentration and drifted onto the sidewalk. Then, when he hit Alex, the shock galvanized him into sobriety, and seeing two bodies in his mirror, he drove off at high speed. While he was negotiating the tricky right-hand turn at the end of the street, he finally noticed he didn't have his lights on. The sequence of events made sense, even though it meant the man was a callous bastard, or just someone scared of being caught mowing down pedestrians while drunk driving.

A police car pulled up beside them. "Are you all right," a plain-clothes officer asked, calling through the window.

"We're fine," Alex said.

"Someone almost killed us back there," Pauline said, feeling the police needed a better response. "A car came up on the path and almost ran us down. We just managed to jump out of its way at the last minute."

The man nodded. "We got a phone call from someone who saw what happened," he said. "Can I take you to the hospital? You really should be checked by a doctor before you go home."

"We're fine," Alex said again.

The policeman got out of the car and stood in front of them, barring their progress.

"You don't look fine," he said. "I can't make you go to hospital."

"Then let us go back to our hotel," Alex said, "where I can clean up these scratches."

"Very well," the man said, "but we were called to an incident. I'd like your names and addresses so we can get in touch in case we need to."

Pauline gave him the information and included her home and phone number. "If the man is as drunk as he appears to be," she said, "you will have another incident on your hands tonight and we might be able to add to any charges."

"Exactly, madam," the officer said, "though I still wish you'd go to a hospital."

"Can we have your name too, please?" Pauline asked. "You aren't a police constable."

"No, I just happened to be nearest," he said, delving into his coat pocket and producing his identity card.

Pauline noted his name, rank, and headquarters. "I'm

glad," she said, "that you're a detective because I want to say something that may or may not be relevant. I think the driver targeted us. It might have been a drunk but the whole thing was odd."

"Why do you think that?"

Pauline frowned, considering her reply. "The way it happened didn't seem like a drunk. It was more deliberate, I thought."

"Did you get the number or make of the car?"

Pauline shook her head. "It was over so quickly. I was trying to get out of its way, and it didn't have its lights on."

The detective nodded. "Well, if anything comes to you when you've had time to think, you have my number. Phone me."

"I will, detective," Pauline read her notes, "Detective Trevelyan. Thank you."

He returned to his car, and with a brief wave, set off down the street in the direction Pauline had indicated the car had gone. Pauline and Alex limped back to the hotel, stopping only at a late-night chemist for supplies. Pauline helped Alex to the bathroom and left her to wash the blood and dirt from her cuts while she poured them each a brandy.

"What made you think the driver was out to get us?" Alex asked, when she limped into the room to rejoin Pauline.

Pauline hesitated, unsure how to respond. "I don't know. Maybe I was just angry," she said slowly. "It was just some-thing you say when an idiot cuts you up. Drink this," she continued, handing her the brandy and antiseptic ointment. "Drink the one and salve your wounds with the other."

Alex sat in an armchair and examined her injured leg.

"You should be more careful with what you say," Alex

said, grinning. "I'm so confused by today I might get these the wrong way around."

"To be honest, the brandy would be as good both ways," Pauline said. "But maybe don't eat the ointment."

Alex sipped the brandy as she smeared the medicated cream across her leg. "It's as well you aren't a doctor," she said with a smile. "Rubbishing your medications that way."

Pauline cut bandages while she watched Alex dab ointment on the worst grazed parts of her calf where the bumper had struck obliquely as she fell. She handed Alex a gauze pad to place over the wound. Alex turned her attention to her thigh, which had been scraped raw by the pavement, and it too was soon covered in gauze. Pauline handed over the bandages she'd cut, and Alex wrapped them around her leg, covering the gauze pads.

"There's up here too," Alex said, shifting sideways on the chair to expose her hip. An angry red circle, which would soon turn blue, surrounded her hipbone; the center of it was oozing blood where the pavement had taken the skin off.

Pauline handed Alex the ointment again. "I'm not a medical professional," she said, "but I can't help feeling Detective Trevelyan was right. You should have gone to a hospital. That looks serious."

"Nonsense," Alex said. "I've had worse falling off a horse."

"Do you ride?" Pauline asked, thinking this a new side of Alex that hadn't been mentioned before.

"Not really," Alex said, ruefully, "which is why I fell off."

Pauline laughed. "Well," she said, "I hope now you'll agree to go to bed and rest. Nothing I said before could persuade you."

Laughing, Alex agreed. "And maybe we won't do as much sightseeing tomorrow as I'd planned."

"I'm not sure we'll do any," Pauline said.

"We Aussies are a tougher bunch than you might think," Alex said. "I may hobble a bit but I'm definitely going to see Buckingham Palace."

"I DIDN'T KNOW there could be this many shops in a country," Alex said when next afternoon they stopped for afternoon tea. "I thought Sydney was big, but this is ridiculous."

"I vote for an end to sightseeing and shopping and we get tickets for a play," Pauline said. Never a keen consumer, she felt her lifetime quota of shopping had been used up in this one afternoon.

"What should we see?" Alex asked.

"For a would-be detective, as you claim to be, it couldn't be anything but *The Mousetrap*," Pauline suggested, then seeing her blank look, continued, "It's a murder mystery. You can practice your detecting from the safety of a theater seat."

"That's a completely different kind of detecting," Alex protested. "There's no murder in my mystery."

"Who knows what secrets you'll uncover or where they might lead," said Pauline in playful seriousness. "That's what makes history so fascinating."

"If you say so," Alex replied sarcastically. "Personally, I think I'll count myself lucky if I find anyone who knows or cares about anything I say."

"I think you'll be surprised," Pauline said. "Here most people care about history because it's all around them and there are lots of restless ghosts who want their story told."

Sadly, Alex was never to get her chance to guess the villain in *The Mousetrap* for the theaters were closed on Sunday evenings.

"It's just as well," Alex said, when the hotel receptionist told them the bad news. "I think now I could sleep for a week."

"It was like that for me too when I flew back here," Pauline said, sympathetically. "We'll lie in late tomorrow and travel up when everyone is already at work."

When Alex was gone, Pauline closed her eyes and went through the details of the accident as best as she could remember. How could a driver lose control and mount the pavement, hit two pedestrians but then re-gain control and drive straight as an arrow away? And then brake for the junction, taking the turn at speed, all without a second loss of control? Nothing, however, came to answer these questions and she, too, retired for the night.

11

THE HEIRESS REACHES LANCASHIRE

Pauline was up early, as she always was, and knowing Alex would probably still be in bed, she returned to the scene of the accident. The thin rain had washed away any blood, but the tire marks were still visible. The car didn't skid, no sign of braking, the marks only showed the sharp turn the driver made when he was sure he'd hit them. Why did she think 'he'? It was most likely, of course. Most cars were owned and driven by men but there was more to it. As the car drove away from them, the silhouette of the driver was visible through the rear window. Yes, a man, and not one with wild hair, no hippie-style or afro on the driver.

Alex didn't sleep for a week, as she'd imagined, but it was late enough by the time she did emerge for breakfast, which they ate in the hotel. This leisurely pace suited Pauline, who wanted Alex to rest and recover. The morning rush hour was well past before they took a taxi to the station and began the trip north.

There could be no thoughts of Alex staying in a hotel now, Pauline had decided, as the train rattled its way north.

Alex may consider what happened an accident, but Pauline couldn't. She knew she was allowing her own experiences of crime to cloud her judgement. There was no evidence of any real criminality here, but her senses said be careful. One way she could be careful was by having Alex safely lodged in her spare bedroom where Pauline could keep watch over her.

"I think it best you stay with me for a few days," Pauline said, as they watched the countryside in its bleak black and gray winter colors flash by. "That way, if you do need medical attention, I can help you get it."

"That's very kind," Alex said. "I'm grateful. I don't know the area which will make it difficult for me to find my way around at first."

They arrived at Pauline's house as the light was failing. It was almost the shortest day, and in the north, that was very short. After helping Alex upstairs with her bags, Pauline suggested she should rest. Alex agreed and Pauline shut the bedroom door as she exited.

When she was sure Alex was staying in her room, and unlikely to hear what was being said, Pauline phoned Detective Trevelyan. Although there was no real reason for secrecy, Alex's volatile personality may take umbrage at what she would see as being coddled by Pauline.

"Good evening, detective," Pauline said, when he answered the phone. "It's Pauline Riddell, one of the two near-fatalities on your patch the other day."

He laughed. "As I recall, Miss Riddell," he said, "I was clearly told you were both fine and it was nothing more than an accident."

"I was making sure you'd remember," Pauline said. "You might not have, as we told you it was nothing."

"I do remember," he said. "Now, have you remembered something that might help?"

"Not really, other than I'm sure the driver was a man. I had a lot of time to think about it on our journey back to Lancashire, you see. What I called about was to learn if there were any similar accidents that night."

"Nothing quite like the one you were involved in," Trevelyan said. "Why are you sure it was a man?"

Pauline explained about the silhouette with its very traditional-looking haircut before saying, "There not being another similar incident that night makes me even more suspicious."

"He possibly drove straight home when he realized how drunk he was."

"Anything is possible," Pauline said. "I just feel it points even more to us being targeted, though I can't see why."

"Mistaken identity, or just a moment of anger brought on by something to do with a woman but not either of you," Trevelyan suggested.

"Yes, yes. I've considered that too," Pauline said. "But none of it quite works, does it?"

"You obviously don't know life in a big city," Trevelyan said. "People here get so angry and lash out at anything. You should see our crime investigations. You wouldn't believe what people do."

Pauline smiled. She could very easily believe what people do. "I'll take your word for it, detective," she said, laughing. "But to this country girl, mistaken identity and blind misogynistic rage don't quite solve this puzzle."

"At least you're back home now," Trevelyan said. "Whatever it was caused the attack you're a long way from it now."

"I hope you're right, detective," Pauline said. "Meanwhile, if anything does transpire, I hope you'll set my mind at ease by letting me know."

She hung up the phone and frowned. All things being equal, the detective should be right. Nothing that happened in London need concern her here.

Another of the ways she decided to be careful with Alex's well-being was in not making the Historical Society immediately aware Alex had arrived in town. She'd told Celia they'd be staying in London to do research this week and Pauline saw no need to alter that impression. Until she could be sure the Society members would behave kindly to Alex, she thought Alex should recover from her injuries first. Alex un-injured was moody enough; Alex still aching from injuries may blow her top if the members' questioning became hostile, though in an English and civilized way, as it had been when Pauline had met them.

Consequently, it was the following Friday evening before she phoned and set up a time for Alex and Celia Ormiston to meet at the entrance to old Cheney Hall.

12

CONFIRMING THE WORST

"This was the entrance to de Cheney Park," Celia
Ormiston said as she and Alex rounded the
corner into a shallow half-circular wall.

Pauline watched them without speaking. It seemed best
to let Alex experience this first real contact with her mother's story without outside commentary. They'd stared at
Buckingham Palace and Tower Bridge together but
somehow that didn't seem like Alex's mother's story any
more than it would be for any other tourist.

Alex stared at the wall and then slowly reached out
and touched it. Pauline could almost read her mind.
Alex was standing where her mother had stood that
morning, the one where she felt her whole life change,
talking to the policeman, trying to see around him.
Pauline saw Alex frown as she realized something
wasn't as the story had led her to imagine. Pauline too
could see the problem; beyond the wall were rows of
ordinary suburban houses where a great house should
have been.

"This can't be the same wall," Pauline heard Alex say,

before going on to explain the differences between the wall she could see and the one her mother had described.

"The Hall was destroyed by the bombs," Celia Ormiston replied, "and they had to lower the wall and take away the gateposts when this became an entranceway to the housing estate. The wall and gateposts were too tall and that made it dangerous for car drivers who couldn't see around them."

Alex stepped out into the road to look through the entrance and down the street between the rows of houses. It seemed to follow the route the drive to the old house must have taken. The street became a T-junction only a hundred yards inside the gate and a mock-Tudor detached house barred her view of anything beyond that.

"What would it have looked like in 1944?" Alex asked.

"We have some photos in the museum," said Mrs. Ormiston. "We can go there after. Basically, what was here was a small gatehouse with iron gates and gas lamps on each post. Looking through the gate, you'd see a fairly short drive – Cheney House wasn't a grand affair like Chatsworth or Lyme Park –bordered by oak trees that met overhead, forming a shaded way in summertime. It may have been nice in summer, but it must have been rather gloomy in winter, I think, particularly as the family had fallen on hard times and most of the outdoor staff were gone by then."

Pauline saw Alex touch the wall again. A puzzled expression on her face. Clearly, she'd imagined old, weathered stones, moss or lichen covered and this wall was another disappointment. The stones were clean and new.

Mrs. Ormiston anticipated Alex's question.

"They are the original stones," she said, "and some of the houses you can see also include stones from Cheney House. It's just they were cleaned when the wall was rebuilt and cleaned again after the Clean Air Act put an end to the burning of coal. Apart from diesel exhaust from trucks and buses, there's nothing nowadays to blacken them."

Pauline watched as Alex walked to the point where the semi-circular wall began and she saw her close her eyes, imagining her mother hurrying along that morning. She'd come from the station, gone now, but Alex and Pauline both knew from Mrs. Ormiston's directions that it would be behind where Alex now stood. Alex's mum couldn't see over the wall. She'd rounded the corner and met the policeman who stopped her before she could reach the gate. Alex walked forward. Perhaps trying to feel what her mother had felt.

"I can show you photos at the museum," Celia Ormiston said. "It would give you a better idea of what it was like then."

Alex nodded. "For a moment," she said, "I thought I was there with mum, in 1944, but then the traffic lights changed, and everything evaporated in the rumble of wheels and the roar of engines."

"I'll visit the churchyard," Pauline said, as Alex and Mrs. Ormiston approached, "while you visit the museum, Alex."

The sepia-tinted photos in the museum confirmed Mrs. Ormiston's words. At the turn of the twentieth century, in summertime, Cheney House was full of life, with tennis parties and croquet on the lawn. By 1944, the house and park had aged considerably, its tennis courts were disused, and the shrubbery had grown wild. Winter photos, in stark, bleak contrasting blacks and grays, looked even worse.

Alex closed the cover on the album and thanked Mrs. Ormiston for her time. "At least," she said, "now I know. I've seen the church with the family history of marriages and deaths; I've seen the remnants of the old house; I've followed Mum down the paths I remember her telling me about and I'm satisfied. There's nothing more to be done."

"You will remember our next Historical Society meeting, won't you?" Mrs. Ormiston said, as she locked the door of the small outbuilding that served as the Old Ashton de Cheney Museum. Alex had agreed to this, against Pauline's strongly worded advice.

"I'll be there," Alex replied, "though I've so little to tell."

"Your mother's story, written up, will be a fine addition to our records," Mrs. Ormiston said. "We have two other descriptions, and the newspaper articles, of the night but nothing as close and personal as this." She held her hand out to Alex who took it, and after a brief shake, turned to go.

"I hope you'll come as well, Miss Riddell," she added.

"Certainly, I'll be there," Pauline said. "My taste for researching is never quite sated."

"Oh, I should tell you, if there's anything else you'd like to see or know, you'll have to phone me after Boxing Day because I'm visiting my sister over Christmas."

"Thank you," said Alex, "but I don't think there will be anything. I think I've seen all there is to see of my mother's story."

"It really is a pity Sir Jocelyn is dead," Mrs. Ormiston said. "Nowadays there are more tests to be done that could have settled your mind one way or the other. The old ways of 'she said, he said' aren't nearly as satisfactory."

"You're right there," Alex agreed.

Pauline also nodded in agreement and thought that in this case, in Alex's mother's case, the 'she said' method was downright slanderous.

They'd agreed to talk over dinner, leaving Alex time to reflect on what she'd seen and learned, so Pauline was forced to wait, though she longed to hear an immediate reaction.

Finally, when they'd ordered and she couldn't contain her patience any longer, Pauline asked, "Did you get anything new from Mrs. Ormiston? She spoke a lot."

"Nothing positive," Alex said.

"Tell me anyway," Pauline said.

"My mother didn't identify the bodies of Sir Thomas and Lady Maud, at least not at the inquest. The doctor did that. In fact, she doesn't appear to have been at the inquest at all."

"That doesn't sound promising," Pauline said.

"I think it confirms what we already knew," Alex said. "Mum was there that morning, her description of the gates to Cheney House is spot on, but not as an important player in the drama. She thought she saw a way to get rich by claiming the de Cheney estate. When she realized her claim would get her into trouble, and a wealthy Australian soldier was offering an easier path to riches, she abandoned the idea and took what was on offer. The story she spun around herself and around me was a delusion she'd created for herself."

"Do you think she would do that?"

"Actually, I think Mum could have done much worse if pushed to it," Alex replied. "She had a temper in her that was frightening to see."

Pauline said nothing. That temper was something Alex had inherited from her mother. They ate their first course in uncomfortable silence. Pauline unwilling to continue with a subject that was clearly depressing Alex and Alex, toying with her salad, looking devastated at the failure of her quest.

When their plates were cleared away, Pauline asked, "What happened to the estate?"

"The Historical Society doesn't do anything past 1945 when the government was still using the grounds as a storage area for old tanks and things. But Mrs. Ormiston said after the government left, which was in the early Fifties, it was the trust who developed the area. With the death of Sir Jocelyn, the trust passed on to two distant cousins."

Pauline felt goosebumps spring up everywhere. "Did she say, 'Sir Jocelyn'?" she asked.

"Yes, of course. She's a very correct lady," Alex replied with a chuckle. "I think all the ladies of the Historical Society are in love with Sir Jocelyn. And I don't blame them. His picture is on the wall and on the desk, one in flying gear and the other in his dress uniform. He was very handsome."

"Never mind that," Pauline said in exasperation, "are you sure she said 'Sir'?"

"She said it on more than one occasion, why? What's the significance in that? He would be Sir Jocelyn, wouldn't he? If his dad was a Sir?"

"No," said Pauline, "he wouldn't. Not until he inherited anyway."

"But he would inherit the moment Sir Thomas was killed," Alex said.

"Only if he was alive."

"Well missing-in-action isn't dead. The ladies are just pretending he's out there somewhere, hoping this handsome knight will come and sweep them off their feet and save them from the dragon of suburban boredom."

"Possibly," Pauline agreed slowly, her mind trying to digest this news and how likely it was to be true, "but I think it means he came back." She remembered the mausoleum's inscription and mentally kicked herself for not seeing it then.

13

A GLIMMER OF LIGHT

"So, what if he came back?" Alex asked, as they drove at racetrack speed through the darkened streets. It had taken forever to get served and away from Christmas Eve restaurant crowd.

"It's the first new information we've heard," Pauline said shortly, "and it means there will be a will. I knew we should have looked."

"It only proves what a liar Mum was," Alex said. "Jocelyn coming back was probably why she abandoned her scheme to steal the de Cheney estate and what decided her to take George Wade's offer."

"Perhaps," Pauline said. "And perhaps he came back much later, and she'd already gone." She pulled up outside the address Mrs. Ormiston had given Alex. There wasn't a light in any window; the house was empty.

"I told you," Alex said, after Pauline had knocked and rung the bell enough times to convince herself the Ormistons were out. "They've gone away for Christmas."

"You're sure they said they'd be back the day after Boxing Day?" asked Pauline.

"She said she'd be back after Boxing Day. She didn't say which day."

Pauline almost wept in frustration. Finally, they had something to work on and now they had to wait for confirmation. She couldn't even follow up with other sources because they too would be on their holidays.

"Why does everything close at Christmas," Pauline grumbled, slamming the door as she got back in the car. "We'll lose a week, you watch."

"If everything didn't close," Alex said, "you'd be at work so you still wouldn't have the opportunity to research." She closed her door gently to emphasize her calmness in the face of Pauline's bad temper.

"I didn't mean me," Pauline replied. "I meant everyone else should work through the holidays."

"Then it could hardly be called a holiday, could it?" Alex continued reasonably. She seemed to be rather enjoying her new role as the steadier one of the two.

"I'm pleased you can take our first real break so calmly," Pauline said, sarcastically.

"It's not a break," Alex replied, "because, like Don Quixote's, this quest was already broken. If Jocelyn came back and left his estate to two distant cousins, there's even less in it for me. Anyway, you know I'm right. My wonderful mother was in the middle of a scam to get his estate when he came back and she had to get out fast, which she did. If Jocelyn was still alive today and I'd presented myself to him as his long-lost daughter, he'd probably have me horse-whipped out of town in true aristocratic fashion."

"I think you're letting your dislike of your mother color your judgment," Pauline said. "For all her later faults, she got one heir to marry her so why not two?"

"She got a drunk, George Wade, who didn't know what

kind of a woman he was getting, to marry her," Alex said, "and I doubt Jocelyn came within a hundred miles of the scheming slut. And..." she added meaningfully, "as far as I can see this break, as you call it, is just more of the same. Nothing my mother said has been true." Alex's sarcastic emphasis on *my mother* was becoming more pronounced as their research progressed.

Pauline, driving at a steadier pace now, considered before replying.

"You know now your stepfather isn't, and wasn't, a drunk," she said, "so he wasn't duped that way if he was at all. And this is a break because what we've heard, seen, and read up to now has been the same story only told from different people's viewpoint. Your mother put herself at the center of the story because that's how she saw it. Nobody else knew she was alive, so she doesn't appear in their version of the story."

"If she was there, surely she'd have been at the Inquest."

"Not necessarily. Didn't you say she went first to the airfield Jocelyn was stationed at? And there was no need for her to be there. The doctor could identify the bodies and what other information did she have to give?"

"None," replied Alex. "That's my point. She wouldn't dare identify herself as Jocelyn's wife or even fiancée then, in case he came back. And, when he did, she ran off to Oz."

"You don't know that," Pauline said as they entered the house, "you only think that. We have to know when he came back."

"*If* he came back, I think you mean," Alex said.

"Right," agreed Pauline but her brain ran on examining and discarding ways for getting information over Christmas. She would start in the morning. Not being at her family home for Christmas, as she was used to, meant there was no exchanging of gifts or preparing of feasts, which freed up a lot of time. With her list of names from the gravestones, which she'd noted when Alex was speaking with Mrs. Ormiston, and the telephone book, she could find some of the old families who must still live in the area.

The following morning, Christmas Day, Pauline ate a hurried Christmas breakfast, handed Alex the present she'd bought when they were in London, thanked Alex for the present she'd brought over from Australia, and then started work. Throughout the night, ideas had come to her, most completely impractical, and she'd repeatedly cursed her weakness in letting Alex avoid the death certificate search when they were in London.

Knowing Pauline's plans, Alex watched with amusement.

"What?" Pauline asked, seeing her visitor's growing smile.

Alex laughed. "Up until last night, I thought nothing could pierce your cool, calm shell and now, at the merest hint of a historical puzzle, you're like a kid with a new toy. The things that finally convinced me of my mother's madness have made you come alive."

Pauline looked up from the phone book and smiled ruefully. "It's true," she said, "I do like a good mystery, one where there are tantalizing glimpses of a different story beneath the obvious one."

"I'm going to luxuriate in the bath," Alex said. "While you waste your time on the phone. You do know it's Christmas morning and no one will be pleased to have you call them when they're with family or making Christmas dinner or whatever?"

"I'm just going to check the phone book, see if some of the families are still in the area," Pauline said. "I'll only call the one or two that seem most promising. The rest can wait until tomorrow."

With Alex out of the way, Pauline began work in earnest, skipping through the phone book and jotting down names and numbers, only one of which she called. Alex was right; the response she received from the person at the other end of the line was not in the Christmas spirit. Accepting the inevitable, Pauline decided she'd only alienate people she might need to interview and that would be a poor way to start. She'd wait until after church and try again.

But after church, her enthusiasm had moderated, and she decided Alex was right. It really wasn't the time. Not everyone thought life had to stop when there was a question to be asked and answered.

"ARE we going to church again in the morning?" Alex asked that evening as they listened to the radio playing Christmas music.

"I was planning to attend the morning service," Pauline said, and then added, "Why?"

"I was just thinking. I tried to stop going to church when Mum died," Alex said, "because it was all part of her life, not mine. Even in that she kept up her pretense. She said we had to set an example to the community, that's what people like us did."

"But now you've found you can't stop?" Pauline guessed.

"I found I didn't want to stop," Alex corrected her.

"If you keep attending with me, in another week you'll be considered part of the congregation," Pauline said, smiling.

"There was a good turn out today," Alex said.

Pauline laughed. "I've been attending when I'm at home for the best part of six months and I saw more people in church today than I'd seen in the whole of the previous time."

"I'm sorry then for the vicar. It must be very disheartening," Alex said.

Pauline, who had strong opinions on the problem with modern church ways, replied carefully, "I'm sure it is, but it is his job to grow the flock, not bore them away."

14

PAULINE'S RESEARCH FRUSTRATED

"Where are you going?" Pauline asked when she saw Alex putting on her coat. Outside it was wet, with a raw wind that had chilled them to and from church that morning. Pauline couldn't see any need to go out in it again.

"I need some air and we need milk and stuff," Alex replied. "You carry on with your research. I'll walk down to the grocery shop. The walk will ease some of the stiffness in my leg."

"I'm coming with you," Pauline said closing the phone book around her notepad. Now that the holiday was almost over and everyone would be at home with nothing to do until New Year, she felt she'd have a better response to her questions. She still hadn't phoned anyone. Her experience on the one Christmas call she'd made was fresh in her mind. She was more used to questioning people who either had to answer or for whom it was in their best interest to answer. Phoning strangers and asking odd questions needed either more tact than she had or more relaxed interviewees.

"If you like," Alex said, "but there's no need. I don't need a crutch. My scrapes and bruises are almost healed, and you wanted to call all those innocent bystanders in my small family non-event."

"Just to be on the safe side," Pauline said, putting on her coat. "I'm going with you. Your leg took a nasty knock. You might need support and I can still phone people after we get back." It was better that Alex thought she was worried about her walking because then she wouldn't be annoyed about Pauline being concerned for her safety. Something still bothered Pauline about that car.

As they walked, Pauline said, "We didn't research the de Cheney wills when we were in London. That was a mistake. We should have done. I'm going to have a work colleague go along to Somerset House and find out if a Sir Jocelyn de Cheney left a will. Failing that, any de Cheney of Ashton de Cheney wills will do. We need that information as soon as possible."

"If you like," Alex said. "We both know it won't help. We know what the will said and how it has been carried out."

"Maybe," Pauline answered. "We just need to have that clarified."

"You think the information the Historical Society people gave us is wrong?"

"Not necessarily, but in my work, we close off all lines of enquiry properly by seeing them through to the end. It's just nagging me that we didn't do a proper job."

"Okay," said Alex said, "but I hope you won't be upset when I tell you I told you so."

It seemed Pauline's fears for Alex's safety were unfounded for they did their shopping and returned to her house unmolested by cars or people.

"You see," Alex said. "There's nothing to worry about."

Pauline smiled. "I'm sure there isn't, but it's best to be safe."

Alex shook her head in amusement. "Shopping isn't so very dangerous you know, everyone does it."

Pauline thought carefully before she replied. Maybe Alex was right. Maybe there was no threat and her own experience of incidents that cropped up during her investigations had led her astray. She would know soon enough for she was expected back at work tomorrow to analyze a set of reports brought in by another of the company's teams who needed a fast turn around and it was all hands to the pumps.

"Nevertheless," Pauline said, finally, "I'd ask you to stay home tomorrow until I return. I know you think I'm mad, but I'm concerned for your wellbeing as much as your safety. Just another day or two to let your wounds heal, that's all."

"Very well," Alex agreed, "if it will make you happy, tomorrow I'll put my feet up and read all this literature about old Ashton."

Pauline was relieved. Alex's words and manner seemed genuine enough and now she could spend the day in the office with an easy mind.

15

NOW IT'S REAL

"Mrs. Ormiston?" Alex asked when she heard the phone picked up. "It's Alex – the Australian heiress." She'd promised Pauline she wouldn't leave the house without her, but the moment Pauline left for work, she couldn't stop herself phoning. That wasn't actually going against her promise.

"Hello, Alex, what can I do for you?"

"I've been waiting until you got back," said Alex, "I hope you enjoyed the visit to your sister?" She listened patiently to Mrs. Ormiston's response, then continued, "I just wanted to confirm when it was Sir Jocelyn came back from the war and when he died." Pauline would be jealous as hell when she told her she'd gotten the answer to the question Pauline had been fretting over these past days.

"It was summer 1946," Mrs. Ormiston replied. "He'd been in a prison camp in a part of Germany given to Poland after the war and the Russians wouldn't let them leave. They were held hostage for prisoner swaps, that sort of thing. It was all part of the Cold War nonsense that was starting around that time."

Alex felt her heart thumping in her chest. Pauline could be right, and she'd been too hasty in giving up.

"And when did he die?"

"Poor man. His time in the prison camps, and he said the Russian one was worse than the German one, ruined his health. He died in 1956. He was chronically ill most of his life after coming home."

"So, did he recover the estate? I presume the government, or someone, must have held it while he was missing?"

"He got some back and got some compensation for land that the government had used for council housing," said Mrs. Ormiston. "You wouldn't know this, but right at the end of the war, the Labor Party won the election and they'd promised millions of houses for the returning soldiers and their young families-to-be. The houses you saw the other day across the road were built on de Cheney land. When Sir Jocelyn got the estate back, he was too ill to run it on his own and it was in such poor repair, he set up a trust to manage the development and at least build better houses, if there had to be houses. Those were the ones you saw through the gates."

"I wish I'd realized this when we were talking," said Alex, uncomfortably aware that once again she'd made life difficult for herself by keeping Pauline out of the quest. She would have asked the right questions.

"I wish I'd known you were interested in what happened later," Mrs. Ormiston said. "We have some pictures and newspaper clippings from the Fifties and Sixties. I assumed you were interested only in your mother's part of the story."

"I was when we spoke," Alex said, "but now I'm getting into the history I'd really like to see those newspaper clippings and photos. Pauline is at work today so I've time on my hands."

"I'm working in the museum this afternoon. Could we meet there?"

"We certainly could, thank you," said Alex. "What time will you be there?"

Alex was almost out of the door when the phone rang. She stopped. Was the call Pauline phoning to check up on her? She'd have to lie about not leaving the house. She waited until she heard the answering machine click and then quietly picked up the receiver. It was Pauline. The message said there was a lot on at work and she wouldn't be home until late afternoon. Alex replaced the handset and closed the front door behind her. Provided I'm home by mid-afternoon, she thought, Pauline would never know.

"So," said Alex, holding up a 1956 newspaper cutting, "a charity and two cousins inherited the trust."

"Yes," said Mrs. Ormiston, "though I hear they never really have anything to do with it. Lawyers run the charity and the trust. The cousins get their share of the profits."

"It says here one of the cousins was a rock star in London."

"Matthew, yes, but that was a long time ago, back in the Sixties. He returned here when the band faded away. These days, he lives in the Ribble Valley quite near his brother, though I believe he still spends a lot of his time in London. Every once in a while, our local paper reports he and/or his kids still live a pretty wild life."

"I should be getting back," said Alex glancing out of the window at the darkening sky. "I didn't realize it was so late."

"You aren't used to our short winter days," said Mrs. Ormiston. "It's only three o' clock. However, you need to be heading back or you'll have a long wait for a bus. The winter evening bus service is practically non-existent."

"Can I use the phone?" Alex asked. "Maybe Pauline could pick me up, if she's home." Now it was growing dark, and she wasn't sure of the buses. Alex felt uneasy.

There was no answer at the house, so she left a message on the machine telling Pauline where she was and that she was on her way home. If she got home first, she would erase it. That thought made her feel guilty. Pauline was her friend, and she was deceiving her for no good reason, and it was not just a spur of the moment deception. This was pre-meditated, planned deceit. She thanked the librarian for her continued help and hurried out into the evening, anxious to catch the first bus that came.

The phone was ringing when Pauline stepped through the door. The phone was in the hall and she picked it up right away.

"Hi, it's me," her London colleague's voice sounded triumphant. It took Pauline a moment to remember she'd asked for his help. "Hi, you," Pauline said, recovering her poise. "Did you find anything?"

"Course I did," the man replied. "I'm not an amateur like you've obviously become."

"Very funny," said Pauline. "Now tell me."

"Only if you ask nicely. Remember, I'll be calling in this favor forever."

"You're pushing your luck," Pauline replied. Jim was a sound man but a bit of a teaser where work relationships were concerned. She was just pleased he was happily married, or she'd always be in a spin with him. "Please tell me what you learned about Jocelyn de Cheney's will."

"Okay but you won't like it. There's no money in it for your friend. The estate is managed as a trust and the trust is left to the De Cheney Fund for Unmarried Mothers but the unmarried mothers only get all the money after two cousins die. While they're alive, the income from the trust is split three ways, the cousins and the unmarried mothers."

"The de Cheney's really had a thing about unmarried mothers," said Pauline, almost to herself.

"Seems like it," Jim replied. "Maybe it was a big thing then, all those Yankee soldiers with nothing to do until D-Day, but in this day and age it's weird. Nowadays it's becoming mandatory to be unmarried if you're a mother. They think it's better to collect money from all men in the country rather than rely on just one."

"Perhaps it's just as well unmarried women want kids because the married ones don't seem to want them anymore," Pauline said.

"Your jibe is meaningless to me," he said. "I'm a happy father of three."

Pauline smiled. He was right, it wasn't him she'd been thinking of. It was someone they worked with. "I've got to go, Jim," she said at last. "Thanks for helping out. And, yes, I owe you. I know you won't let me forget."

"You can count on it," he said.

For a moment, Pauline was taken aback. There was an edge to his answer she'd never heard in his voice before. She shook her head. She had to stop seeing, or in this case, hearing, everything as suspicious or she'd go mad.

THE BUS STOP was busy with women boasting of the bargains they'd gained in Boxing Day sales, and commuters returning from work. Alex watched them all, imagining their lives, reveling in their gruff accents, so different from the Australian high-pitched 'Strine'. She even loved the misty darkness, the damp stones shining in the streetlamps, and all the other things Wadeville, Australia, didn't have.

The bus, when it finally picked them up, meandered through back roads, stopping frequently, emptying as the town receded behind it. Even sitting at the back, Alex could hear the driver muttering curses at the dark-colored car that either followed too close or dawdled under the bus's nose all the way from old Ashton to Whalley center. By the time the bus reached Alex's stop, there was only Alex and two other women on it. Alex hoped the other women would be getting off too because even the short walk from the bus station to Pauline's house seemed risky now that daylight was gone. Her insides fluttered in fright when the women stayed in their seats as she alighted.

Alex looked up and down the street. Commuter traffic rushed steadily both ways. Whalley was a quiet village for England but a pedestrian nightmare to someone used only to Wadeville. Alex limped hurriedly across the street when a gap appeared in the cars, conscious of her aching leg. It seemed much worse tonight and the butterflies in her stomach added to her discomfort. She wished now she'd waited for Pauline and promised herself she'd listen to the ever-so-gentle-but-firm lecture she would get. The village, empty of people, with its tall Victorian homes lowering sinisterly over her, seemed to hold its breath as Alex began walking up the street, leaving behind the lights and roaring traffic, entering the quieter part where Pauline lived.

The lane was so quiet she heard immediately the footsteps behind her. Heavy, men's shoes, not the click-clack of women's wear. Forcing herself not to look around or increase her pace, Alex walked on. She'd lose him when she turned into Green Lane, the short path that joined Pauline's street to the one she was on. The man followed her into the lane, his pace matching hers, neither gaining nor falling behind. Alex began to tremble, her heart pounded in her chest, and she found it hard to breathe. His footsteps echoed in her mind. It was like every murder mystery movie she'd ever seen, the mist, the darkness, and the narrow lane with its thick privet hedge barring any escape.

Alex was quickening her pace when she saw Pauline appear at the end of the lane. She opened her mouth to call out, then her head snapped forward and she was falling down with a searing pain in her head into a deeper darkness.

"Hey!" Pauline yelled as she ran toward Alex and the shadowy figure that had suddenly pounced and struck her. The man, startled by Pauline's cry, grabbed at Alex's purse but it was caught under her shoulder. Foiled by her dead-weight on the leather strap, he turned and fled back toward the main street.

Pauline skidded to a halt beside Alex's still form. She knelt down on the wet cobbles and checked her pulse. It was steady, there was no sign of bleeding, and she breathed a sigh of relief. Looking down the lane, she saw the figure of a man, silhouetted by the lights of the main street watching her.

"Get help," she called. "Police and ambulance." The figure moved off without a word and she and Alex were alone again. Pauline placed her coat over Alex, not daring to move her and unable to leave in case her attacker returned. Cars passed each end of the lane, but no one came. Pauline grew desperate. Alex was growing colder as the mist turned to drizzle and she still wasn't responding to her voice or gentle touches.

A group of girls, chattering loudly, entered the lane. They stopped when they saw Pauline and Alex's inert body.

"Get help," Pauline called. "We need the police and an ambulance."

The girls huddled together, whispering. Then two went back out of the lane and two approached Pauline warily.

"What's the matter with her?" one asked.

"She's been attacked and hit on the head," Pauline said.

The girls, still wary, stayed out of Pauline's reach, watching her for signs of latent violence, until a police car entered the lane and illuminated the scene with its headlights.

The police were as suspicious as the girls had been and Pauline had to travel in the police car to the hospital, where they watched carefully while she paced back and forth in the corridor. The coincidence of her supposed arrival in the lane at exactly the moment Alex had been attacked sounded lame to Pauline and she wasn't surprised the police thought so too. Their questions were politely incredulous when she persisted in saying it was the truth.

Alex recovered consciousness slowly and it was an hour or so after she arrived at the hospital before the doctor allowed her to speak to the police. To Pauline's relief, she remembered the events leading up to her attack. The police were satisfied and Pauline was able to visit Alex's bedside, but the doctor's opinion of Alex's case was less happy. Alex was to stay in the hospital overnight for observation. Pauline went home alone, despondent. Her fears for Alex's safety, which had seemed so unlikely after Jim's phone call, now appeared justified, though she still couldn't understand what was going on.

16

NO MOTIVE BUT A SUSPECT

A part from a headache, and a very un-Australian paleness, Alex seemed unharmed when Pauline picked her up at the hospital the next day.

"You look fine," Pauline reassured Alex when she was asked for her opinion.

"England's an exciting place," Alex said, getting into the car. "I've never had so many serious incidents in one week. First being mowed down by a drunk driver and now knocked out by a mugger."

"It seems odd, doesn't it," Pauline said, "but it can't be anything to do with your quest because,"

"I know," Alex interjected, "the estate was left to two cousins."

"Is that why you were out alone?"

Alex blushed guiltily. "Sorry," she said. "To be honest, I thought you were nuts, imagining there was someone out to kill me. Now, the coincidence of these two events has made me a bit scared. I know it can't have anything to do with the will, but something strange is going on. I'd be pleased to have you as my escort for the next while."

"You're right, it can't be the will," Pauline said, and recounted to Alex what Jim had told her.

"Then what is it?" Alex demanded. "I don't know anyone here."

Pauline frowned. "Maybe there was something left outside the will?"

"If that's true, it still doesn't explain it."

"I think we have to assume someone knows something and your presence has unnerved them," Pauline said.

"And I know who it'll be," Alex said. She told Pauline what she'd read in the newspapers. "One of those cousins is doing this. My money is on the rock star because I've just remembered, Celia Ormiston told me he lives here and in London, so he had the opportunity."

Pauline laughed. "I don't like rock stars either," she said, "but we have to consider. If this person thinks you can take whatever it is from them, they must know you are actually descended from the de Cheney's, which we know is really unlikely."

"Well, he has some motive, that's for sure," Alex said. "All we have to do is find out what it is. I didn't get to play detective at *The Mousetrap* show you promised but I am going to get to the bottom of this. This second attack has given me fresh hope."

"I'm pleased to have you aboard," Pauline said. "The first attack caught my attention."

"We'll be a detective team," Alex said, "like they have on TV." She paused, her eyes shining, and then added, "You know, I don't think I've ever felt this alive."

"Well, partner," Pauline said, "if you plan to keep *being* alive, from now on you go nowhere without me, or someone else who understands the risk."

"I see that now," Alex said, "and I'll stick to you like glue but what do you say to my idea? It must be him, mustn't it?"

"We can easily check his location, I would think," Pauline said thoughtfully. "Someone like him will have plenty of people watching. Someone in the village will know if he's here or in London right now and if he was in London when the first attack happened and here when the second one happened."

"Who would know?"

"The local newspaper for one," Pauline said. "Celebrities are always good for articles and sales. We'll visit their offices tomorrow, check their back issues, and grill whoever is in the office."

"Won't they be suspicious?"

"Not when they learn you are a great fan, and being over here on vacation, you're hoping to get a glimpse or an autograph," Pauline said.

"I don't like rock music and I don't know what group he was in," Alex pointed out.

"By the time we've read the back issues, you'll know everything you need to know to sound like a fan," Pauline said. "And where there's something you don't, put it down to you growing up so far away in Australia."

"You do seem to have a talent for this," Alex said. "It's just a pity we don't have someone who knows how to really do detecting. We could use some actual expertise."

"We'll be just fine," Pauline replied. "We have all the expertise we need, and we can call on detective Trevelyan for assistance at that end."

"Would he help us?"

"We can ask," Pauline said. She didn't add they would ask right after she'd spoken to Inspector Ramsay and have him make the introductions. When Alex had retired for the night, she was still finding the time change irksome, so Pauline called her old friend.

17

THE ROCK STAR AS SUSPECT

Fortunately, for their investigation, the local paper's offices were open, and they were allowed access to the back issues. They pored over article after article going steadily back in time tracking the interesting life of the local bad boy, who didn't seem so very bad in Pauline's mind. The scandalous behavior the paper recorded would hardly have made it to the gardening page if the man hadn't been a moderately well-known member of a briefly famous group in the Sixties. The groups fame had flared and died within a very short span, not even five years. There were so many groups like that. They rode on the coattails of The Beatles, The Rolling Stones, and one or two other groups who'd burst out of the UK onto the international stage, but The Shades of Blue had crashed and burned before exit velocity had been achieved.

"There isn't enough in these later articles to say where he is or where he has been these past two weeks," Alex complained.

"No," Pauline agreed. "In fact, the paper seems to have lost interest in him and his family these later years. Either the man has set lawyers on the paper or the family is just boring nowadays."

"Then I'll have to do my long-time-fan-dying-to-know-where-my-first-crush-is-now routine," Alex said.

Pauline nodded. "I'm afraid so," she said. "Did you have a favorite pop star? If you did, try to focus your mind on them when you speak."

"Mother liked Tom Jones, I remember," Alex said.

"It has to be someone *you* liked," Pauline said, a little exasperatedly, "or you won't get the feeling right."

"The kids who tormented me at school all had their favorites, stars they loved," Alex said, "which only made me hate all of them."

Pauline sighed. "Just do your best," she said, "and don't consider acting as a career."

Alex looked shocked. "I never would," she said. "They're no better than the rock stars."

The woman at the desk, however, didn't need any prompting to talk about the local celebrity. Unfortunately, what she had to say wasn't conclusive. He might have been in London before Christmas and he might be home now. The paper no longer took much interest since he'd settled down to being a local businessman and member of the golf club.

"Well," Alex said, disgustedly, "what now?"

"We can go and look at his house," Pauline suggested. "That may show if the family is at home."

The rock star's house was an upmarket, modern building set among trees outside of town with similar homes for its neighbors.

"I'd been hoping for something more traditional," Alex said, as they stared through the locked wrought iron gates at the end of a short drive. An intercom box was located on a gatepost. "Can we think of an excuse to call, do you think?"

"Charity is always a good excuse, anything to do with Africa gets rock stars excited. There's a lot of public relations mileage there." Pauline's recent investigative work had included a nice little money earner for the owners of just such a scheme.

"Where would we get the leaflets and stuff?" Alex asked.

"You're the detective for this case," Pauline said. "Where do you think?"

Alex pondered, then brightened. "The library had lots of brochures and leaflets for charities," she said.

"Excellent," Pauline said. "We'll drop in there on our way home. After lunch, we can try our luck."

THEIR LUCK WAS IN, it seemed. The security man who answered the call, after hearing they were collecting for orphans in Africa, transferred them through to the rock star's wife.

"We don't allow canvassers up to the house," the woman said. "I'll send a donation down to the gate with Arnold, our security man."

"Thank you," Pauline replied, trying to sound pleased. "I wonder if it would be too much to ask another favor?"

"Such as?"

"I have an Australian friend staying with me and she is such a fan of your husband, has been since their first record. Would it be too much to ask for an autograph?"

"My husband doesn't do that anymore," the voice said. "We're all too old for fan worship, I'm afraid."

"Oh," Pauline said, sadly. "That's disappointing. Is your husband there? Just to say hello?"

"I'm afraid he isn't here right now."

"Never mind," Pauline said. "We see your security man on his way so thank you for the donation. We'll take up no more of your time."

"What are we going to do with the donation?" Alex asked, as they walked away from the gates and were safely out of the security guard's hearing.

"Put it in the Water for Africa donation box in the library," Pauline said, "or any one of the others of your choice, if you prefer."

"Meanwhile," Alex said, "we're no further forward. Is he away from home or just out at some local meeting, do you think?"

"Oh, just local, I'd say. Isn't here 'right now' were her words," Pauline replied.

"What can we do now?"

"We can watch and wait," Pauline said. "Right here, I think." She crossed the road with Alex following. "We can see their gate from here and we'll be reasonably well hidden."

"But it's freezing, and everything is wet, the branches, the ground, everything."

"You won't have to wait long," Pauline replied. "I'll walk back and get the car. There's a place we can park on the other side of the entrance to their property. I'll come back and pick you up. It won't be more than fifteen minutes."

"I'll have pneumonia by then," Alex groaned.

"You exaggerate. You'll have little more than bronchitis, though that is what most Britons die of I believe. It's a wet climate all year round."

"Wet? I've never seen so much water in my life," Alex said.

"You'll be pleased to know then it's been a dry spell over

the past weeks," Pauline said, unsympathetically. "Now, keep your eyes peeled on that gate until I get back."

"I'M numb from my head to my feet," Alex said, when Pauline stopped her car at the curb and opened the passenger side door. She flopped gratefully into the warm car and closed the door quickly.

"Did you see any vehicles enter the property?" Pauline asked, ignoring the complaints.

"Only a baker's van."

"Good. Then we'll park a little way along here and watch in relative comfort," Pauline said.

"I wish you'd brought my book," Alex said, when an hour had passed, and they were still watching and waiting.

"When it happens," Pauline replied, "you won't have time to look up from a book and take in the details. You have to be aware all the time."

"It's growing too dark to see any details," Alex said.

Pauline had to admit that was true. In a very short time, there'd be no hope of recognizing a driver in a car at this distance.

"I think this might be him," Pauline exclaimed, before she'd have to agree with Alex. A silver Aston-Martin, the model James Bond had made famous, was slowing as it prepared to turn into the gate.

Both women leaned forward, peering through the glass and the growing darkness to identify the driver. The car turned and stopped at the gates.

Pauline put her own car into gear and drove slowly past the entrance where the sports car and driver were waiting for the gates to fully open. Through the Aston-Martin's side window, they got a glimpse of a jowly, round face.

"No wonder he doesn't want his fans to see him," Alex said as they continued toward home. "He's grown fat."

"Are you sure it was him?" Pauline asked. She was sure. He'd filled out a lot, it was true, but it was still the same man she'd seen in the newspaper photos that morning.

"Oh, yes. I'm sure. He's older, balder, and fatter but it's him all right."

"You're very censorious," Pauline said with a laugh. "He's older, that's true, his hair is receding, that's also true, and he's filled out but he's hardly obese."

"I don't like rock stars," Alex reminded her.

"A woman after my own heart," Pauline said. "Now, we know he's here today but not that he was here when you were attacked, and we don't know if he was in London when you were attacked there."

"How will we find that out?"

"That is going to be trickier," Pauline said. "People don't unfortunately come with tags to follow. We find the local busybody. She'll know."

"Who's that?"

"I don't know but I suspect Celia will, so we start there."

They called Celia the moment they returned home. It took a moment before Celia was comfortable passing on a name and she only did this after Alex once again went through her speech about being a fan of the group since she bought their first record. Armed with a name and some background, Pauline called the number she'd been given. Again, it took a moment or two before the woman would pass on what she knew. When she did, however, both Pauline and Alex were delighted to find their suspicions confirmed.

"I knew it," Alex said. "He was away from home before Christmas and back for the holidays. Now what do we do?"

"We call detective Trevelyan," Pauline replied. She called but had to leave a message as he'd gone home for the night.

"Could he really help?" Alex asked. "We don't know where the cousin stayed or very much about him. How will Trevelyan know where to look?"

"We know the car and its number," Pauline said. "He may be able to get information from that. Now we have dinner and think about our next steps."

18

THE GAME IS AFOOT

Trevelyan called them back early the next morning. After the detective described the phone call he'd had with Inspector Ramsay and congratulated Pauline on her expertise as relayed to him by the said inspector, he asked what he could do for them. Pauline gave him the license number and described the car she was interested in.

"We hope you can give us some information about where he was just before Christmas," she said, finally.

"Only if this car was illegally parked or disobeying a traffic rule," Trevelyan said. "What is this about, Miss Riddell? I can't use police resources to help you buy a new car."

"Quite so," Pauline said. "But I'm not trying to buy a new car. The owner of this car may have been the person who tried to run us down."

"You will have to explain why you think this," Trevelyan said.

Pauline explained what they'd learned and how it was

possible the owner of this car may have a reason, as yet unknown, to want Alex gone.

"Hmm," Trevelyan said, "that is a lot of ifs and possibilities. Are you sure?"

"I'm not sure," Pauline said, "but I think it worth exploring."

"Inspector Ramsay vouches for you," Trevelyan said, "So I'll do it this time, but you will have to find better reasons than this if you want more."

"So, what now?" Alex asked, when Pauline hung up the phone.

"We find out what the other cousin has been doing these past days," Pauline said. To herself she thought, *and I'll learn more about the mysterious Fund for Unmarried Mothers when I get to work on Monday.* The company library and resources would easily show if the charity existed and who to talk to about it. A call from an internationally known accounting office generally either loosened tongues or silenced them, but a call from a potential donor was always treated with respect.

Going back to work rather worried Pauline. It would leave Alex alone. They had to do as much investigating as they could over the next three days and hope they discovered enough to allow Alex to stay indoors out of harm's way. She suggested this. Alex however would have none of it.

"I'm not a child," she said indignantly, "and you are not my guardian."

"I didn't mean it like that," Pauline said, hoping to quell what she saw as Alex's too easily roused temper. "I'm only concerned for your safety."

"You needn't be. I've suffered two unexplained accidents, which are likely entirely unrelated to me or anything to do with the de Cheneys. I think you're making me as paranoid as you obviously are."

"Perhaps, you're right," Pauline said. "This really has nothing to do with me and I've let my enthusiasm carry me away. Shall we forget all this nonsense and do some sightseeing instead?"

Though she was still flushed and clearly upset, Alex nodded. "You made me long to see the Lake District. Why don't we go there?"

"Get your hat, coat, gloves, scarf and the sturdiest boots you have with you," Pauline said. "I'll provide the umbrellas. There's a reason those lakes are where they are."

Alex laughed. "I grew up hearing nothing but droughts. You can't show me too much water."

"I think I can," Pauline replied. "Let's go."

Their day wasn't as wet and windy as it could have been, Pauline thought, as they drove home soaked through and steaming up the car's windows, but it was pretty close.

"It's beautiful," Alex said, when Pauline sounded like she was apologizing for the weather. "The mists in the valleys, the snow-covered peaks, the flashes of sunlight when it broke through the clouds, it was all so atmospheric. It's like a tale of long ago come to life."

"Atmospheric is exactly what it is," Pauline said, sarcastically. "I've yet to visit on a day that wasn't atmospheric, as you put it."

"It's as I told you about Wadeville," Alex said. "You have to be an outsider to see the beauty."

"Oh, I see the beauty well enough," Pauline said. "I just prefer my beauty to be tamer."

Alex shook her head. "Beauty can't be tame, only quiet sometimes."

"Is that a quote?" Pauline asked suspiciously.

"I don't think so," Alex said. "Sometimes, I surprise myself. Too long thinking only my own thoughts, I suppose."

"Do you have anything you'd like to do tomorrow?"

"Go back to The Lake District again," Alex said. "That's a place to visit often. It's a place where you can believe in the old gods as well as the true one. When we saw that cloud appear from out of nowhere, I swear I expected to see Vikings appear too."

Pauline laughed. For a whole day, their focus had been on keeping dry and warm as they'd followed muddy pathways through forests and along the shores of wind-whipped lakes and all without a thought to wills or suspicious characters.

There was a phone message when they reached Pauline's house. Pauline listened.

"Trevelyan says he'll call later," she told Alex. "And he says there's no speeding or parking record for the cousin's car in London any time in December."

Alex shrugged. "I've been thinking about it and he wouldn't use his own car, and such a conspicuous one at that. It would need repairing or cleaning after, wouldn't it? The garage would be able to bear witness against him, if questioned."

"No," Pauline agreed, "he would most likely take the train to London and rent a car down there or use taxis. We just had to be sure, though. That's how research is."

"This whole idea is a wild goose chase, you know," Alex said. "The will has been read, the beneficiaries have their rightful shares, and none of it includes a mention of my ridiculous mother."

Pauline nodded. She was glad Alex was beginning to forgive her mother enough to at least see her as ridiculous which was better than the anger she'd shown before.

"I recommend you have a hot bath while I prepare dinner," Pauline said. "Warm you through, ready to brave the elements again tomorrow."

The phone rang as Pauline busied herself in the kitchen. It was detective Trevelyan, as she'd hoped.

"You got my message?" he asked.

'I did," Pauline said. "There was never a high probability he'd have broken the traffic laws just to suit my convenience, but it needed to be checked."

"Do you have any other ideas?" Trevelyan said, before adding, "Ideas that don't include using police resources on fishing expeditions, I mean?"

"I have some," Pauline replied coolly, not rising to the bait, "which I'll follow up at this end."

"You don't think you have it all wrong?"

"Honestly, everything says I have. Even the victim now thinks I have, but something's not right. I know it."

"And your instinct is never wrong," Trevelyan said, with a laugh.

"Sadly, my instincts frequently lead me astray," Pauline said. "Which is why I carefully sift through all the evidence I have before coming to a final conclusion."

"You don't have a clean-up rate metric to meet," Trevelyan said. "The public likes their judgements swift, first, and correct, a distant second."

"Are you and Inspector Ramsay related?"

"No, why?" Trevelyan laughed.

"For a moment, you sounded like him, that's all."

"Reality comes to us all in time, I guess," Trevelyan said. "Even you, Miss Riddell, will one day begin to question the essential goodness of human nature."

'I have the bible to remind me of the true nature of human beings, detective," Pauline said. "It condenses all the observations of hundreds of people over thousands of years and warns us what to expect if we fail to guard against our own nature."

"If we're straying into religion," Trevelyan said, "it's time for me to go. I just wanted to be sure you understood I can't help you further unless you have something clearly criminal for me to address."

"I do understand," Pauline said. "Thanks for your help on the car and I hope we won't have to bother you again." She replaced the handset, deep in thought. It would certainly be best if nothing unusual happened and Alex saw what she came to see and went home satisfied. In the meantime, she had dinner to make.

19

IT FEELS LIKE HOME

"It's New Year's Eve," Pauline said, as they drove north to The Lakes once again. Today was clear, bright, and frosty, in stark contrast to yesterday. "I hadn't anything planned to mark the New Year's arrival. Have you anything you would normally do that you'd like to do?"

Alex shook her head. "Mother and I never celebrated it. I wouldn't know how."

"Then we'll stay in and listen to the chimes of Big Ben on the radio," Pauline said. "Much better than parties or gathering around outdoor clock towers in this weather."

"Is there a clock tower?"

"Not here," Pauline said. "I have a friend Poppy who lives in Morpeth, it's up in Northumberland and nothing to do with my life really. Only, these past few years, I've taken to joining her around the clock tower there. It's very jolly, everyone comes out of the pubs and waits for the clock to chime in the new year."

"It does sound better than sitting at home alone."

Pauline laughed. "It is, when you know everyone. If you

don't, you can feel lonelier in a crowd than in your own home."

"I suppose that may be true," Alex agreed, doubtfully. "Still, I'd like to experience it for myself even if it was just once."

"I've just realized," Pauline said. "You told me you'd seen your mother's birth certificate and I forgot to follow up with you on that. We talked of more immediate things and it slipped my mind."

"There's nothing to tell," Alex said. "She was born in Manchester. There was no father on the birth certificate."

"And her mother, your grandmother?" Pauline asked. "Did you look for her in the deaths section? She may still be alive. She may have had brothers or sisters and you may have cousins."

"I didn't have time," Alex said. "I will look on my next visit to Somerset House, but I think the fact mother never mentioned them, not even once, tells me all I need to know. Either she wanted nothing to do with them or there were none."

"You're probably right," Pauline said. "She may have been placed in an orphanage or with a childless couple. Those were common things to do in those days."

"I've been going over this in my mind a lot lately," Alex said. "If it was something like what you say, and she was unhappy all her childhood, I could be more forgiving toward her. If she simply rejected her family, I'll be even more angry with her. It's an odd sensation, not knowing how to feel about my own mother."

"I imagine all of your recent experiences must be unsettling," Pauline said, nodding. "She was a strange character, your mother."

"God save us from strange parents," Alex said, laughing.

"They're all strange," Pauline said. "It's just a matter of how far they fall outside the circle of being normal."

"My mother was a long way outside," said Alex, suddenly serious.

The seriousness was lost as soon as they parked the car and began their ascent up to the heights of Skiddaw. Frost gave way to snow as they climbed steadily along the well-marked path. Other walkers seeing out the old year with a last trek on the high ground wished them Happy New Year and Alex's eyes shone. Her whole appearance became more alive. While Pauline thought it an odd response to a freezing, mournful-sounding wind and snow-covered earth, she could understand it. The view over the lake far below, to the snow-covered peaks beyond was enough to raise the spirits of the most melancholic of souls.

"My father may not have been Jocelyn de Cheney," Alex said, when they once again paused to take in the view, "but he came from here somewhere. This feels like home to me."

"Perhaps you come from a long line of Lake District shepherds," Pauline said.

"Standing here, I can believe that's true," Alex said. "Do you really think what has been happening to me is a coincidence?"

Pauline thought. As so often in their time together, Alex would come out with seemingly random questions that showed Pauline exactly the tortuous paths her mind had been following. Now, if she said she did think they were coincidences, Alex may go home and the threats to her life might end. If she said she didn't believe they were, Alex may continue her own investigations and be killed.

"I don't believe in coincidences when the outcome is a monetary advantage to someone," Pauline said at last.

Alex nodded. "I agree. I belong here. I know I do and I'm going to find out how," she said.

"It will be dangerous," Pauline said, "you know that, of course."

"I've had two strong hints to remind me," Alex said.

"At home, we had a board game when I was a child," Pauline said. "It was in the form of a knight's quest. Around the edge of the board were mottos, encouraging bravery. The one I remember best was 'Faint heart ne'er won fair lady'. We're very modern knights you and I, but nevertheless, we too need brave hearts."

"I think I have to go on," Alex said. "If I'm such a threat to someone, then even going back to Australia won't save me. As long as I'm alive, I'm a risk to them, whoever they are."

"I hoped returning to Australia would keep you safe," Pauline said, "but your deduction is a valid one. They may feel they have to go on until the threat, which is you, is eliminated. Shall we go down and find lunch? I'm freezing."

"You should have dressed for the heights," Alex said, enjoying a moment of superiority. "I'm toasty warm."

They began descending, back along the trail they'd followed up. They were a long way from the two summits of Skiddaw and Alex, taking a long wistful look back at the peaks, said she'd come back and reach both when the weather permitted.

"It's just as cold in August," Pauline said.

"I don't believe you," Alex said, "at least not about this. Are you going to continue researching that rock star cousin?"

"I will assist, if you wish," Pauline said, warily. "Remember, I'll be at work starting Tuesday and you're on your own."

"You really haven't been listening, have you," Alex said. "I've always been on my own and often in fear of being attacked. Mentally speaking, I'm trained for this."

Pauline nodded. "I think you are," she said. "Then, yes, we go on."

It was dark by the time they reached Pauline's house and snow was beginning to fall. Pauline was glad Alex didn't want to go out and celebrate New Year's Eve. They scurried inside and locked the door behind them.

After a late dinner, they listened to music on the radio until the countdown began. Pauline topped up their glasses of sherry. When the chimes ended, and they'd toasted to the start of 1978, a successful outcome to their investigation, and repeated Nelson's toast of 'confusion to our enemies' they climbed the stairs in that bittersweet mood that accompanies the end of one year and the birth of another.

20

NEW YEAR, NEW RESOLUTION

After church, with the obligatory wishing Happy New Year to everyone in the congregation, they walked up through the wooded Whalley Banks to the Nab, a bare peak with a wide view over the village and valley.

"How are we going to prove it was the rock star?" Alex asked Pauline as they admired the view.

Pauline chuckled. "It's your investigation," she said. "As I said, the best way is to find the motive. When we know that, we'll know who."

"How do we do that?"

"The Historical Society may have a copy of the will or they may have knowledge of bequests that were made outside the will."

"We should talk to Celia again," Alex said.

"We should but that will have to wait. She's away again." Pauline's tone made it very clear how little she appreciated this constant absence of their principal source of local knowledge.

"Too many holidays," Alex said, nodding seriously. "The country is going to the dogs."

"It is and there are too many holidays," Pauline said, smiling in spite of herself. "So, we'll do what any sensible person would do when there's nothing to do except walk out in this freezing wind. Go home to a nice fire and lunch." She set off back the way they'd come.

"I can't help thinking," Alex said, "that you and I were somehow switched at birth. You long for sunshine and heat and I for greenery and a fresh breeze."

"You forgot the rain," Pauline said. "You don't get to be called a 'green and pleasant land' without a lot of rain."

"You're proving my point," Alex said, "with every word you say."

They continued their back-and-forth chatter until they reached the bridge and the main street, which they seemed to have to themselves.

"Apart from that man fiddling with his car," Alex said, "everyone in the village is at home."

"It's Sunday and New Year's Day," Pauline said, "which makes it doubly a holiday. Everyone is tucking into their roast beef Sunday dinner. We won't have anything as cheery, I'm afraid." As she spoke, she kept her attention on the one man that Alex had mentioned. He looked familiar but a name for him wouldn't come and before they'd come close enough to discern his face clearly, he'd jumped into his car and driven away. She recognized it's receding rear at once. Now she was sure Alex was in some form of danger. That was the car that hit them, she was sure of it. What make and model of car it was, would take some research to discover.

For Pauline, this new national public holiday of New Year's Day, which had been only a local day off in the north when she was a child, was seriously irksome on this occasion. A few years before, she'd have been able to go into work today and research the Fund for Unmarried Mothers who were benefiting from the de Cheney will. As it was, she was obliged to ferry Alex to more local sights.

"For tomorrow," Alex said, "I'm taking your advice and taking the train to Manchester and its library. I'm looking for *Who's Who* and any up-to-date book on local companies and their directors. Is that right?"

"It is," Pauline said. "It's painstaking research, trust me on this, but with luck you'll find all we need to know about our rock star businessman. I'll drop you at the station on my way to work."

Alex grimaced. "The library won't be open so early, surely," she said.

"You have to use transport, buses or trains, filled with people," Pauline said, "or get a taxi and don't let anyone share it with you."

"You're doing what exactly, while I'm working?" Alex asked.

"I'm working for my employer, exactly," Pauline retorted. "If you're going to be a detective, you have to learn some detecting techniques."

"These techniques sound more like forensic accounting techniques to me," Alex said. "Movie and TV detectives don't do anything like this."

"It wouldn't be much of a movie, if they showed this part," Pauline said, "and this isn't a movie. It's real life, which requires real work, so get to it."

"I'm having my own detective agency in the future," Alex said. "My partner in this one is a tyrant."

21

ALEX AND PAULINE INVESTIGATE
SEPARATELY

P auline had told Alex she was going to be working for her employer and she was, for the most part. However, she was certain the company library had a copy of registered charities, and when she searched the shelves, she found she was right. She'd never had to investigate a charity since taking up her present position, but she knew one team of the company's accountants was doing just that.

The register showed the Fund for Unmarried Mothers was in good standing and paid out a steady stream of revenues to deserving cases. The payouts were growing small, which suggested there was very little left of the de Cheney family fortune by the time Sir Jocelyn had died.

After a brief, unsatisfactory spell at her desk trying to get into the actual case she was working on, Pauline couldn't resist returning to the library to see what the *Companies Register* said about the rock star cousin's directorships. Again, everything looked normal. Nothing jumped out as being suspicious, which in itself could be construed as suspicious to a suspicious mind, she acknowledged to herself ruefully. She returned to her office thoroughly out of sorts with life and her own mind. Fortunately, a scheduled meeting with her fellow team members passed the rest of the day with enough stimulation to drive all her doubts out of her head.

As she drove home through the evening rush hour, her thoughts returned. The two events that had led her to think that behind Alex's mother's strange story there must be a kernel of truth could easily be just one of those incredible coincidences that happen in real life and. And, as Alex had rightfully said in her angry outburst, she was not her guest's guardian. By the time she arrived home, Pauline had finally accepted this was not a case for Miss Riddell, sleuth-extraordinaire, and she would stop behaving as though it were.

As she entered her house, Alex called from the kitchen, "Welcome home. I hope you like meat pies?"

"I do. Why?"

"The butcher's shop was open, and he had pies in the window. Australians love their pies, you know," Alex said. "I had to have one to see how they tasted here in England, but I couldn't decide which one and bought one of each. You choose whichever."

Pauline smiled. "When I was driving around the Blue Mountains, I heard one radio advertisement for pies, over and over," she said. "How did it go?" She paused, trying to recall the jingle.

"Football, meat pies, kangaroos, and Holden cars," Alex sang. "That one?"

"Yes. That one," Pauline said. "I didn't know pies were such an icon of Australian culture. I thought it was lamb."

"It is lamb and it's also meat pies, many of which are made of lamb," Alex said. "You don't seem to do that here."

"It's true, ours are basically beef," Pauline said.

"Well take your pick. I'll have the rest for lunches this week while you're working."

As they ate, Pauline gave Alex a rundown on what she'd learned that day in the company library.

"It's very useful having all this financial information on hand," Alex said.

"I have found it so on many occasions," Pauline said.

"However, I'm pleased it has convinced you there's nothing sinister going on around this nice village or around me," Alex said. "I can stretch my legs, now they've stopped aching, and really feel what it's like to live here. It's very different."

"You mean it rains a lot," Pauline remarked, dryly. "What did you learn at the library?"

"Oh, that," Alex said. "Nothing. That book, *Who's Who*, gave me plenty of information that said nothing about him being a homicidal, embezzling maniac and the *Companies Register* for this region said even less."

"How long did you stick with it?" Pauline asked, and was pleased to see the guilty expression that crossed Alex's face before changing to brazen defiance.

"Long enough to convince me I'd find nothing there," Alex said. "So, I came back here."

"I thought your legal secretary work had trained you in searching documents," Pauline said, smiling.

"That doesn't mean I enjoy it. In fact, I plan never to do that again. I'm too full of life now to be stuck with dry, dusty documents."

"Roughly translated," Pauline said. "You were bored."

"That too. What I mean is, a lot of people in the village already know who I am, and they say hello, and ask how I'm enjoying my stay. I've never had that happen before and I'd rather spend time with them than with books."

Pauline hoped her expression didn't show the sorrowful dismay she felt at Alex's simple statement, which said so much about her life.

"I'm pleased people are being hospitable," Pauline said. "We Brits are famous for being stand-offish."

Alex nodded. "I know and maybe to someone with a different background than mine, they actually *are* being stand-offish but to me everyone seems very kind and thoughtful."

As Pauline had wondered how Alex was going to fill her days while waiting to talk to the Historical Society before traveling back to London, this news was a relief.

"I am glad," she said. "It could have been very lonely for you wandering the streets without anyone to talk to."

"When I got back from Manchester, I went into the teashop for afternoon tea and I was invited to sit with a group of mothers," Alex said. "One of them is the daughter of a member of the Historical Society so she knew all about me and I spent almost an hour telling them about Australia." She paused, frowning, and then added, "I'm not sure they'll have a good picture of life in Australia because I've seen so little of it."

"Never mind, they've seen even less," Pauline said, smiling. "What of tomorrow? Have you given up on your quest?"

"Ha," Alex said triumphantly, "you think I wasted my day and got nothing done. I knew you would. What if I told you, I learned more in two minutes chatting in the teashop than I learned all morning in the library?"

"I wouldn't be surprised," Pauline said. "What did you learn?"

"One of the mothers, Janice I think," Alex paused, trying to recall, "knows the woman who *does* for the rock star. She can give us a day-by-day account of what he does and where he goes. Now what do you say?"

"I say you did well," Pauline replied. "When are you going to meet her?"

"I hope tomorrow, maybe the next day. It depends on when Janice can get her to the teashop, really."

"And how are you going to handle this interview?" Pauline asked, fascinated by this energized trainee detective she was raising up.

"I thought I'd stick with the fan-since-my-teenage-years story," Alex said.

"Then I suggest you do your homework tonight and tomorrow morning. Find out everything you can about them."

Alex frowned. "How?" she said. "The library's closed now."

"That's where I can help again," Pauline said. "I have some books and magazines that will have bits about them."

"Were you a fan of rock music? You don't seem the type."

Pauline laughed. "I was not, and am not, a fan, but I did some work on an earlier investigation when I first joined my present company. It was an investigation into music and entertainment contracts. Normally, I would have thrown all the papers out, but I was re-assigned to the Australian investigation and they're still upstairs. I'll get them." She left the room, returning minutes later with an armful of papers, magazines, books, and loose papers.

"Are you sure the rock star in question is among all that?" Alex asked, grimacing.

"A lot of these are just industry papers," Pauline said. "They're gossip for the most part. There's a good chance your rock star and/or his awful band gets a mention somewhere." She dropped the papers on the table. "All yours."

Sighing, Alex took a seat at the table and began sorting through the mound, separating the magazines from the papers and books.

Pauline, smiling smugly to herself, picked up her book and prepared to settle down for the evening.

"Pauline," Alex said, breaking into her quiet, "you'd tell me if you didn't want me staying on, wouldn't you? I can go to a hotel, you know."

"I'm enjoying having some company," Pauline said. "Don't even think you're not welcome. However, I think it's a shame, for your sake, the Historical Society weren't meeting tonight. Then you could have that meeting behind you, and you could begin your vacation properly." Tuesday was the usual night for the Society's meetings but this week it had been canceled to accommodate those who'd gone away for the holidays.

"I don't mind," Alex said. "I'm enjoying my stay. I could stay here forever."

Pauline hoped she didn't look quite as dismayed by this as she felt. It was nice to have company and it would also be nice to have her house back.

They returned to their evening pursuits, which suited Pauline because she had spoken to Celia by phone that day and found another source of information. She intended to follow up on her way back from work the next day and was busily imagining all the questions to ask and how best to ask them.

Despite her stated dislike of the pop music industry, Alex found the magazines fascinating and constantly interrupted Pauline with cries of 'did you know?' until Pauline wished she'd never given them to her.

As they prepared to retire for the night, Pauline asked,

"Is Janice bringing the woman who *does* for the rock star to the teashop tomorrow?"

"If she can," Alex said.

"Make sure you have the dates and places clear in your mind when you meet her," Pauline said.

Alex sighed. "I'm not entirely hopeless, you know. I'll be ready."

Pauline laughed. "All right," she said. "I'll stop fussing. Good night."

22

OLD LOYALTIES

It had rained all day and was still drizzling by the time Pauline, huddled under her umbrella, rang the doorbell of a small cottage surrounded by houses on the edge of the village. The cottage must have been a pleasant, private place until new houses crept around it.

The curtain of the bow window to the right of the door was pulled aside and an elderly woman peered out. She obviously decided Pauline was safe for, in a minute or so, Pauline heard bolts being drawn and the door opened.

"Miss Quigley?" Pauline said. "I'm Pauline Riddell. I hope Celia Ormiston spoke to you."

"She did. Come in out of the rain, dear. You'll catch your death."

Pauline stepped inside and folded her umbrella to place it in the old-fashioned umbrella stand behind the now closed door. Miss Quigley took her coat and hat, hanging them on wall pegs above a drip tray.

"Have a seat," Miss Quigley said. "I'll make us a cup of tea. You'll want warming up, I'm sure."

As Pauline's car heater was in good working order she

didn't need warming up, but over a cup of tea was how one talked so she said, "That would be lovely, thank you." And followed Miss Quigley into a small living room.

"I won't be a moment," her hostess said, making her way through another door to where the kitchen must lay.

Pauline heard the kettle being filled and the lid of a teapot being lifted. A moment later, Miss Quigley was back.

"It won't be long," she said. "Celia said you were interested in Sir Jocelyn after he returned to the village. Is that right?"

"Yes," Pauline replied. "I have a guest staying, she's from Australia, and her mother said she knew Sir Jocelyn as a younger man."

"I heard about your guest," Miss Quigley said, grinning. "Quite put the cat among the pigeons by all accounts."

"Sadly, Alex's mother seemed to have told her a story that poor Alex, being a child, took to be true. She told the story to me when I was working out there and I, not knowing anything about it, asked the Historical Society and it did, as you say, create quite a stir."

"Her mother claims she was engaged to, or even married to, Sir Jocelyn before he was shot down, I believe."

"That's correct," Pauline said, "and nobody had heard of such a thing."

"Those folks are good with their books," Miss Quigley said, sharply, "but not so great with people."

"You must have spoken to the ladies of the Society many times, I expect?"

"I did, once or twice and then I stopped," her hostess said. "They were rude, in my opinion. I was Sir Jocelyn's cook and housekeeper for ten years and they, who hardly even met him, would tell me I didn't know anything."

"Historians are keen to have written sources," Pauline said.

"And what are written sources if not the words of people?"

Pauline decided it was time to return to her purpose for this visit. "You, who knew him so well, must know if he said he was engaged or married."

"He was a man of his time," Miss Quigley said, "which means he didn't share personal information or grief easily."

"Not once in the time you were working for him?"

Her hostess shook her head. "You have to understand. I was staff not a family friend," she said. "He was always kind and gracious toward me, always, but we weren't bosom pals."

"If you didn't hear anything of that, then I think we must conclude it really wasn't true," Pauline said. "I was afraid that was the case, but poor Alex has taken it badly, learning that her mother constantly lied to her throughout her whole life." It wasn't exactly the truth, Pauline thought, but sympathy may elicit more information than direct questioning.

"Poor dear. I do understand. We all look up to our parents, don't we? To catch them out in a serious lie, not a nice story like Santa Claus, must be awful."

"How did you come to be Sir Jocelyn's right-hand woman?" Pauline asked.

"I began work straight from school in Cheney Hall, as a parlor maid. I was very ambitious and had great hopes of becoming housekeeper there in due course," Miss Quigley said, smiling. "It was the year war broke out, the first one, I mean."

"So, you knew Sir Jocelyn as a child?"

"Oh no," her hostess said, shaking her head. "That war,

and what came after, did it for the Cheney family's invest-
ments and most of the staff were let go shortly after the war
ended. Me among them. I got a job at the mental hospital
where wartime shell-shock victims were being looked after.
Sir Jocelyn was born after I'd left the family's service. I don't
rightly remember when. This was all a long time ago." She
lapsed into silence, her mind far back in time.

"And you were at the mental home when Sir Jocelyn
came back? Was he a patient there after the second war?"

Miss Quigley shook herself and continued, "Oh no, it
was the Depression that put an end to the mental home,"
she said. "It lost its funding and closed in 1933, if I remember
right. I was lucky and got a job cooking at the boys' school,
Stoneyhurst. I loved it there. A nice class of gentle folks'
children. I was still there when I heard Sir Jocelyn was
home. He'd taken a bungalow on the new estate that was
being built and needed a cook and housekeeper."

"And that was when?"

"It was 1947 and oh what a terrible winter we had in my
first few weeks with him. Sir Jocelyn kindly ran me home in
his car more than once. He was a wonderful man."

Again, she'd drifted into a reverie of long ago, leaving
Pauline frustrated at the slowness of the tale. Particularly as
they'd now reached the crucial time period.

"You said how much you liked the boys' school," Pauline
said. "Then what made you decide to change?"

Miss Quigley smiled. "Many reasons. One I told you, I
had ambitions to be the Cheney Hall housekeeper," she
said, grinning. "Cheney Bungalow may not have been quite
as grand as Cheney Hall, but it was almost as important. Sir
Jocelyn still entertained and needed a skilled cook and
housekeeper." She paused, before continuing, "And also I'd
been at the school fifteen years. It seemed like time for a

change. Most of all, though, it was affection for the de Cheney family. My mother and father worked at the Hall all their lives and had nothing but praise for them."

"Was it your connection to the family that tipped the balance in your favor for the position, do you think?"

"Possibly it was. It couldn't have been the interview I had with Sir Jocelyn because it was very sad and solemn," her hostess said. "I thought after that I'd not shown my best."

"Why?"

"We talked about my parents, who'd recently died, and especially his memory of my father, who'd been kept on when the indoor staff were reduced. And he remembered hearing my fiancé had been killed at the end of the first war. He asked if I'd found another. I hadn't and we talked about that. He quoted Jane Austen 'women love longest even when all hope is gone'. I hadn't read Jane Austen then, nobody I knew had, so I went to the library after, and in the years since I've read all her books."

"I too remember those words," Pauline said. "Even Jane says it is not a quality she'd wish on anyone."

Miss Quigley nodded. "I agree," she said. "My father died two months before my mother. I was with her at the end and her last words were, 'I'm coming, Bob,' in the cross tone she always used whenever they went out and he was waiting patiently, and quietly, for her to check everything in the house before locking the door. She was such a fusspot; you wouldn't believe, but he understood. Now, I too feel that pull across the divide growing stronger daily."

"Perhaps Sir Jocelyn understood your feelings about your parents," Pauline said. "He'd so cruelly lost his own when he couldn't be near them. Perhaps that was what he wanted, someone who understood his feelings, as well as a cook and housekeeper."

"I think it was too. There were so many pert young women after the job, and more besides."

"Did Sir Jocelyn leave any bequests outside his will, do you know?" Pauline asked.

"He left me a generous gift, but I don't know if anyone else received anything," Miss Quigley said. "Why?"

"I don't rightly know," Pauline said. "It was just something someone said, and it puzzled me."

"If it was one of the old biddies in that Society," Miss Quigley said. "I should take it with a very large grain of salt. They're that jealous of each other they can't bear anyone else having a story to tell."

Pauline thanked her for her help and took her leave. What she should tell Alex of this was Pauline's concern as she drove home. If Sir Jocelyn never once mentioned a fiancée, let alone a wife, to Miss Quigley, it was almost certain there wasn't one.

Her concern was misplaced. Alex was in high spirits after a day spent chatting to what seemed like everyone she met in the village. Pauline couldn't help feeling a twinge of jealousy that Alex had been here a week and was bonding with everyone while she, Pauline, had been here months and knew no one.

"Miss Quigley's information says no more than we knew," Alex said, when Pauline told her what she'd learned.

"There's something," Pauline said. "I think you should go back to Somerset House and get a copy of that will and any documents associated with it."

'Why? We know what it says," Alex exclaimed. "Even your friend from work saw nothing in it for anyone but the three named beneficiaries."

"It's possible there's information in the will that points to other documents or something like that," Pauline replied.

"Something must be yours and someone has it and that someone is trying to hold onto it. In which case, it's valuable."

"Your friend would have mentioned that, surely," Alex said.

Pauline shook her head. "We have to study that will ourselves," she said. "Having others tell us about it means we're getting their interpretation rather than the truth."

"You want me to go back to London," Alex said.

"Yes, and I think you should do that as soon as you can."

Alex frowned. "I like it here," she said. "It feels like home and I've only been here a few days."

"You could be there and back in a day," Pauline said. "Two at the most."

"I could, couldn't I?" Alex said, brightening. Then she added, "But not until after tomorrow evening because the Historical Society have invited me to meet them. Celia said they promise to be on their best behavior. What do you think she meant by that?"

"Researchers can get very pushy sometimes," Pauline said, earnestly. "When I met them, they certainly were, and Celia was concerned they would be the same way with you."

"Oh dear," Alex said. "I may get angry."

"You do tend to be defensive about your story and life," Pauline agreed. "But now you know you do, and know they can be pushy, you'll be able to cope."

"Certainly I will," Alex said, rolling her eyes.

Pauline smiled. "That's the spirit," she said. "By the way, I assume Janice didn't produce the woman who *does* today?"

Alex shook her head. "Maybe tomorrow," she said.

23

ALEX GOES WALKABOUT

W hen Alex joined the afternoon tea group next day, there was an older woman seated at the table and she was delighted to find it was the daily woman who looked after the rock star's house. Janice made the introductions and Alex told the woman her now well-practiced tale of how thrilled she'd been to learn one of her favorite rock group's members was living here in the village.

She was preparing to embellish her tale by repeating the snippets she'd learned from Pauline's papers and from the library shelves that morning when the woman said, "He hates that time of his life, you know."

Alex was momentarily taken aback. How would a devoted fan react to learning her idol now rejected everything his fans still loved?

"Why?" she asked, playing for time.

"It almost killed his eldest boy," the woman said. "The kid took to drink and drugs before he was even a teen, encouraged by the stories of his dad and by his dad's drug-addled friends who came to the house. He threw everything out and got his kid into rehab. None of that life gets into the house now."

Alex nodded solemnly. "I can see how that would change someone," she said. "Well, I'm glad I didn't see him in the street and gush all over him like a teenager."

"You'll not see him much around town," the woman said. "Nowadays it's only business and vacations that get him out of the house."

"Not even a Christmas or New Year's party?" Alex asked. "That shows amazing self-discipline."

"Oh, we had both at the house," the woman said, "but only family and close friends."

"If only I'd known," Alex said. "I was here before Christmas. I could have gate-crashed like a groupie." She laughed to show she wasn't serious.

"He was in London before Christmas so you couldn't."

"But I was in London too," Alex said, excitedly. "I landed the weekend before."

The woman shook her head. "That's when the party was," she said. "The seventeenth. He went to London on the Monday after."

"I'm fated never to meet my schoolgirl crush," Alex said. "I see that now."

"It's for the best," the woman said. "As I said, it upsets him, all that nonsense."

"It was nonsense, wasn't it?" Alex said. "When I look back at myself then, I wonder if I was quite right in the head."

The woman laughed. "Then?" she said, "I'm still that way over Engelbert Humperdinck."

Alex left the teashop and walked home, deep in thought.

Her disappointment was crushing. She'd been so sure it was him and now it had to be the other cousin. Her thoughts drifted to the Historical Society meeting later that evening. She needed to show confidence and not be wallowing in self-doubt.

At the hastily convened meeting of the Historical Society that evening, Alex related her mother's story while the ladies took notes, asked questions, and taped the whole session. Alex was nervous. Although she still believed her mother's story was a lie almost from beginning to end, she now believed some part of the history must be true and it made it a hard story for her to tell. Some of the questions didn't help.

"Your mother claimed she was Sir Jocelyn's wife, or was it fiancée?" A thin faced woman asked in a tone that set Alex's nerves tingling.

"She said both, but now I don't believe either was true," replied Alex, a little defensively. She didn't dare tell them her mother had assumed the even more elevated title of 'widow' on her marriage license to George Wade.

"Sir Jocelyn never mentioned her to any of us, you know," another woman interjected.

"Or anyone else, so far as I can tell, which is why I now believe she was making that part of the story up." Alex dug her fingernails into her palms to stifle the angry retort she was longing to make.

"She wasn't a local girl? We might be able to learn something about her if you knew where she was from." A different woman this time but the tone as sharp and, Alex felt, sneering as the previous ones.

"No, she wasn't local. Her birth certificate says Manchester, but where in that city, I'm not really sure. She never mentioned anything except her part in this story."

"Didn't you think that odd?"

"I was just a child, so I didn't think much about it. It was just there – Mum's story. Did you question your parents about their lives?"

"Actually, most of us did. We're interested in that sort of thing."

"Well, I wasn't," Alex replied stubbornly. She could feel her temper rising and took long, slow breaths to calm herself. Looking around the table at the sharp eyes of the committee members, she felt she was being grilled by a host of hostile lawyers in a trial for her life.

"Had your mother visited the house before? Did she say anything about her time with Sir Jocelyn that we could follow up on? Maybe that way we could help you find answers." Yet another pointed question. This one seemed to suggest they'd take over from here.

Alexandra bristled with rage. Now they wanted to muscle in on her quest. What was it with these people, she thought angrily, didn't they have any sensitivity at all? *My family, my quest, my investigation, and that's the way it's staying.*

"Nothing that I can recall," Alexandra replied coldly, "but thank you for the offer." An offer she was sure was intended to uphold the purity of Sir Jocelyn and make her mother out a liar. It was one thing to know you're descended from a scheming gold-digging slut but having someone else prove it publicly was a step too far.

The interview ended and Alex walked back to meet Pauline in the nearby coffee shop as arranged. Inwardly she was fuming. The overcast sky and thin cold drizzle echoed her mood on a grander scale. She'd had it up to here with nosy Brits, cold wet weather, and overbearing so-called friends.

"How did it go?" Pauline asked.

"Fine," Alexandra said sullenly.

Pauline looked at her, puzzled. She'd gone to the meeting nervous but in good spirits, now she was angry. She may or may not be Jocelyn de Cheney's child, but she was certainly her mother's daughter, Pauline thought not for the first time.

"What went wrong?"

"Nothing."

"Something has upset you," Pauline persisted.

"It's nothing to do with you," Alexandra replied.

"They weren't as well-behaved as they should have been," Pauline guessed.

"I need some air," Alexandra said, her voice rising as fast as she rose from her seat, "and some space. This is about my family and I'll sort it out for myself." She stalked out of the café, slamming the door behind her.

When Pauline arrived back at her car, Alex wasn't there so she settled down to wait. Many people were still on vacation and trying to find Alex in the crowded street filled with traffic and bargain-hunters, in the failing winter light, would be next-to impossible. Sooner or later, Alex would cool off and return to the car. She didn't have anywhere else to go.

When an hour slipped by and Alex still hadn't appeared, Pauline decided it would be best to go home. After all, Alex may already be waiting there. She wished now she'd chased after Alex instead of giving her time to cool off.

She started the engine and drove slowly down the street, looking into doorways or other hiding places as she went by in case Alex was sheltering in one of them. She wasn't, nor was she at home when Pauline arrived there. By the time she'd prepared the evening meal and Alex still hadn't returned or called, Pauline was growing worried. First the car, then the mugging, now this... disappearance – if that was what it was.

Pauline phoned the Ormiston house. "I'd like to speak to Mrs. Ormiston, please," Pauline asked the man who answered the phone. "It's Pauline Riddell." She tapped her foot nervously against the coffee table leg as she waited for Celia to come to the phone.

"Yes, Miss Riddell, what is it?"

"What happened to Alex at the Historical Society?" Pauline demanded, her nerves making it impossible to indulge in the usual small talk.

"Nothing happened," Mrs. Ormiston replied, puzzled. "Why?"

"When she returned, she was in a foul mood, and after yelling at me, stormed off. I haven't seen her since. I'm getting worried."

"Well, I don't think it was anything to do with us, Miss Riddell," Mrs. Ormiston said. "She was perfectly rational when she left. I could tell it had been a strain for her, answering a lot of questions, everyone is so eager to help, but I assure you she didn't seem upset when the meeting ended."

Deeply unsatisfied at this response, Pauline put down the phone. The moment she did, it rang. She picked up the handset, "Yes?"

"Hello, Pauline," she heard Alex's voice say.

She breathed a sigh of relief. "Where are you?" Pauline asked.

"I'm in a restaurant called The Taj Mahal," Alex said. "Do you know it?"

"I'm afraid I don't," Pauline said. "Where is it? I'll come and pick you up." She heard Alex asking the waiters for the address and wrote it down when Alex relayed it to her.

'I'll be there in fifteen minutes," Pauline said. She put down the phone, grabbed her coat and hat, and practically flew through the door to the car. She wanted to give Alex as little time as possible for changing her mind and disappearing again.

The weather, however, had turned snowy. Fat flakes splatted on the windshield as she drove slowly through the darkness. Her heart was heavy. What had started out as a simple, fun investigation to lift her spirits after that bruising case in Australia had become a truly sad tale of misunderstandings and disappointment. Alex may have thought she hadn't believed her mother but on some deep level she must have done, and this was the result. And Pauline hadn't understood the depth of Alex's disappointment.

"Thanks for coming," Alex said, when Pauline burst into the brightly lit Indian restaurant to find her sitting by the door. "I don't have a coat and hat and the weather is awful now."

Biting her tongue to quell the sharp response that was hovering just there, Pauline said, "You can't have walked all the way here, surely? It's miles."

"I'm a good walker," Alex said, despondently. "Just not good at much else, it seems."

"Never mind that now," Pauline said. "Let's go."

"I owe the restaurant for my meal," Alex said. "I came without my money."

Pauline thought the waiter nearby had only been anxious for Alex's well-being. She now saw he was waiting to be paid. She went to him to settle up, but he waved away her money. She thanked him and, as she turned to go, the man said, "Is your friend well?"

"I think she had an unpleasant experience," Pauline explained. "She'll be fine when she's warm and home."

"I hope so," the man said. "She came in out of the storm and seemed not to know where she was or how she got here. We aren't near any houses she could have walked from and she had no car. She wouldn't give us a name or number to call."

Pauline nodded. "Thank you for looking after her," she said. "I think it's just the cold. She'll thank you herself when she's recovered."

Pauline wrapped her coat around Alex's shoulders and got her in the car as quickly as she could. The snow was still falling, and the drive back seemed interminable.

"I'm sorry about dragging you out on a night like this," Alex said suddenly.

"Don't worry about it. You've clearly had a severe shock and you're not quite yourself."

"Have I?" Alex asked. "I don't know. I got so cold. They were very nice."

"They were," Pauline said, laughing. "Not everyone would take in and feed someone who was clearly unable to pay."

Alex smiled. "It's true. I think they were a bit frightened to be honest. They probably thought I was mad."

"Walking around without a coat, hat, waterproof boots, and umbrella on a night like this would tend to suggest someone not quite in touch with reality."

"I didn't mean to stay out," Alex said. "I just thought I needed some air and space and I'd be fine. But I walked down the street, over the bridge, and then, instead of turning back, I just kept walking."

"Can you tell me about it now?" Pauline asked, afraid of what the question might make Alex do.

"I'll try," Alex said. "When Mum was gone, I swore I'd never again take notice of anyone's wishes but my own. But you were so helpful and knowledgeable, I felt safe with that. Then tonight the ladies of the Society were so ruthlessly competent, I found myself thinking of you all as trying to take charge of me and mine."

Pauline thought this unnerving. "You thought I was bossing you about? I didn't realize I was so overbearing."

Alex shook her head. "You're not really," she said. "I can't explain except to say, I felt you were all taking over my life and my *quest*, and I got scared, I guess. I'm not used to so much attention."

"You don't think you might have over-reacted a little?" Pauline asked, with a laugh she immediately regretted at seeing the pain on Alex's face. "I'm not laughing at you," she explained, "only my own lack of understanding."

"Perhaps I did over-react a little," Alex said, "or maybe even a lot. I'm sorry."

"You don't need to apologize," Pauline said. "It is your life, your quest, after all. I'm just glad you phoned."

"There is something else," Alex said.

Hardly daring to hear what it was, Pauline said, "Oh?"

"It wasn't the rock star."

"You know that for sure?" Pauline asked.

Alex nodded and explained what she'd learned that afternoon.

"That does seem to put him into the 'innocent' side of the ledger," Pauline said, "but it isn't the end of the world."

"To you maybe," Alex replied. "I'd got him locked up in prison with the whole of the world praising me for my brilliance on TV and radio and in the press."

"Great detectives always suffer a setback or two before they solve the crime," Pauline said, as she drew her car into the driveway and switched off the engine. "Let's get you indoors and warmed through before we talk anymore."

After a hot bath, and wrapped in a heavy robe, Alex sat in front of the gas fire sipping warm Ovaltine while Pauline waited anxiously to learn more about what had brought about this alarming brainstorm. To her own prosaic character, none of it made any sense. She could only listen and hope to understand.

When Alex didn't begin, Pauline said, "Were the ladies of the Society so very bad?"

"Maybe not," Alex said. "How can I tell? Why do you think women have such shrill voices? It really isn't nice. Especially in a group."

"You don't find the women in the teashop shrill though, do you?"

"Not when I'm there, but now I think I might."

"The two events, learning it wasn't the rock star and the ladies grilling you might have been too much for one day," Pauline said.

"What does that say about me?" Alex said. "You would have shrugged them off and I couldn't stand them."

Pauline laughed. "You should see me after a bad meeting at work," she said. "I stalk around the house for hours trying to get over it."

Alex shook her head disbelievingly. "I'm sure you don't," she said. "Anyhow, what is clear to me is my whole reason for being here is nonsense. We know the will was implemented years ago, we know the only real possible villain is innocent, we know for sure now I'm not the child of Jocelyn de Cheney. It's over. I think that's what I was struggling to come to terms with."

Pauline thought carefully before saying, "There's still the other cousin."

"No. I'm finished with all that. I've met with the Society and told them all I know. I can go back to

London and do some more sightseeing before going home."

"A wise decision," Pauline said. "I recommend an early night and take tomorrow to say your goodbyes to the mother's group before leaving."

"I'll do that," Alex said, rising from her chair.

"We'll talk again in the morning before I leave for work."

24

ALEX KNOWS WHO IT IS

When Pauline left next morning for work, she was sure Alex was going to London and then Australia and her decision was final. However, on returning home that evening she found her mercurial guest had changed her mind.

"I don't understand," Pauline said, when Alex had told her she was staying for another few days.

"I'd forgotten in the disappointment of finding the rock star innocent that you said we should see what the other cousin was doing," Alex said. "I'm quite proud of myself. Today, at the teashop, I asked the gang and now I know where the other cousin lives. Tomorrow, I'm going to do some real detecting."

"Even though you were sure yesterday there's nothing to detect?" Pauline said.

"I know, I know," Alex agreed. "It's just I missed detecting today. Real detecting, I mean, not your bookish kind. Talking to people you hear things, and today has given me a new burst of energy."

"Be sure not to be caught alone in some out-of-the-way place, Alex," Pauline said. "Stay safe."

"I thought you'd decided there was no danger."

"I think it's highly unlikely you are in any danger," Pauline said, patiently. "Still, two odd things have happened, and you can't ignore that."

"Detectives can't be concerned with possible danger, or they'd never do any detecting, would they?" Alex said, airily.

"They're paid to take the risk. You aren't," Pauline said.

"Ah, but the detective we've talked to says he can't act unless we give him some proof of criminal activity," Alex said. "And as I'm the person things are happening to it's up to me to find out why."

"I haven't given up entirely," Pauline said, "as I told you this morning. I just think it would be better for us to be very low-key and reduce the risks."

"You have your real work to do. I don't. I'll have it sorted out before your 'slow and steady wins the race' gets out of the door, you'll see."

Pauline sighed. "What do you plan to do?"

"I'm going to do a stakeout outside his house tomorrow," Alex said.

"We could do it together," Pauline said. 'It would be warmer in the car."

Alex shook her head. "No," she said. 'I'm back on top of my game again. You do your own investigating."

"Dress warmly and stay out of sight," Pauline said, shaking her head. "Now, let's forget all about it for tonight."

Pauline spent the day on the usual weekly chores, all the while wondering how Alex was faring. The day was showery but not snowing. Alex had told her she was going to watch from a café across the street from the cousin's house.

As she hadn't expected to see Alex until dinner time,

Pauline was surprised to see her marching grimly up her short drive to the door only shortly after lunch. She looked thunderous and Pauline's heart sank. She liked Alex but her moods were wearing.

"Well?" Pauline asked, when Alex had flung off her coat and burst into the living room where Pauline was sipping her tea.

"He's innocent," Alex said tersely.

"How can you determine this after only one morning's viewing from the opposite side of the street?" Pauline asked.

'You've never seen a more down-trodden, hen-pecked man in your life," Alex said. "If he was to murder anyone it would be his wife and I for one would be a character witness for him. What a witch!"

"What on earth happened?" Pauline said, laughing, but bewildered by this much outrage at such a small glimpse into someone's family life.

"The family left the house, it was pouring down by the way, and got into the car," Alex said. "In that short space of time she berated him constantly, while he got the kids inside and settled. Once she was inside the car, she sent him back to the house for something she'd forgotten. I doubt their son will ever marry or wish to."

Pauline laughed. "You don't know what happened before this took place so it's hard to know the context," she said.

"No one should treat their partner that way in front of their children, whatever happened before," Alex said, firmly.

Pauline was about to respond and then realized Alex was remembering all the instances she'd been berated by her own mother and watched her mother berating her father too. It was best to give Alex's mind a different focus.

"Then it's possible it's the wife who is trying to remove

you," Pauline said. "After all, her lifestyle depends on the money as much as his does."

"Oh. I never thought of that," Alex said.

"Because you'd allowed your anger to stop your thinking. You must stay detached, if you hope to solve mysteries."

"You're right," Alex said, nodding. "I was so angry. I haven't thought of anything else the whole way home. My blood was boiling."

"Once you'd cooled off, you'd have come to realize it," Pauline said, encouragingly.

"Now I need to know where she was," Alex said. She paused. "But didn't you say it was a man you saw both times?"

"It was," Pauline agreed, "but he may only be the instrument. The brains behind this may be someone quite different, like a desperate wife."

"If it is, I've been wasting my time chasing these cousins," Alex cried.

"They are the most likely to benefit from your death," Pauline said. "You have eliminated one of them from your enquiries, now you must be sure about the other – even as you cast about for other possible perpetrators."

"Oh, Lord," Alex said. "It could be anybody."

"Now you've gone too far the other way," Pauline said. "Keep your focus on the will and your possible part in it. If there's skullduggery going on here, it's something to do with that."

"I could spend a lifetime chasing shadows here," Alex said.

"It's true, you will spend your remaining life chasing shadows – if they murder you in the next little while," Pauline said, adding, "and if I don't murder you first."

Alex laughed. "You must find my wild swings of emotion annoying, being so cool and rational yourself."

"I hadn't noticed," Pauline lied. "Honestly."

"Seriously, though, how am I to prove his wife is trying to kill me?"

"You don't know she is," Pauline protested. "I just said she was another possible suspect. You haven't ruled out the hen-pecked cousin, have you? His very weakness may be what's driving him. Imagine what his life would be like if he lost the cashflow from that trust?"

Alex shuddered. "Poor man," she said. "You're right. He may be desperate enough to try murder to escape the wrath of that gorgon of a wife he has."

"That's better," Pauline said. "You're seeing possibilities where you saw none before."

'Now I come to think about it," Alex said, "in one way I can believe it is him. The attempts on my life, if they were attempts on my life, were amateurish. The sort of thing I could imagine a weakling like him doing, rather than something his altogether more competent brother would do."

"The same is true if it's the wife," Pauline said. "She will have found someone she can manage, a family member down on his luck perhaps, rather than a professional."

"I feel better already, knowing I'm up against an amateur," Alex said. "I'll do another stakeout tomorrow after church."

"The café won't be open," Pauline reminded her. "I suggest we sit in the car."

25

A STAKEOUT AND CONFRONTATION

The stakeout was as tedious as such things are, but it did give Pauline the opportunity to find her views aligned with Alex's on the subject of the cousin.

"Poor man," Pauline said, as they watched the family go out for a Sunday afternoon walk in the freezing wind and the wife talking at him with only brief breaks when she snapped at the children instead. "I think it's her voice and sharp features that make her so shrew-like."

"She barely draws breath," Alex said, as they listened to the monologue while it passed them on the other side of the lane.

"They aren't as well off as the rock star's family," Pauline said. "They would feel the loss of the trust money more."

Alex nodded. "I think they're quite hard-up," she said. "The house and garden need work and they aren't dressed in the latest fashions. Not even the kids, which I think is telling."

"You have a good eye," Pauline said. "Yes, they may be desperate enough to eliminate you and incompetent enough to do it badly. Their car isn't the one I saw that night, so it isn't them directly, I think."

"I'm going to get her alone and accuse her," Alex said. "That should speed things up."

"Watch and wait, first. We may see the car arrive at their house or something of that kind," Pauline said. "Sunday's the day families get together, after all."

"Oh, I didn't mean today," Alex said. "It would be during the week when the kids are at school and he's at work. I'll knock on the door, introduce myself and accuse her of trying to murder me."

"It's a bold plan," Pauline said. "Be sure you have a brick in your purse, in case it comes to fisticuffs."

"I can take care of myself," Alex said, "especially with a mousy creature like her."

Pauline shook her head and hoped her own investigations would turn up something solid soon because Alex hadn't the patience needed for this task.

"You will just watch and wait today, won't you?" Pauline asked as she prepared to leave for work. "There's a long way to go before you can successfully confront either him or her."

"Yes, yes," Alex said. "You fuss like an old woman. I'll do as we discussed. Watch from the café and look out for a man in a Wolseley or Riley car." When Pauline had watched the car driving away in the street only days before, she'd taken the time to discover the make and model. Unfortunately, though not hugely popular, it was sold under two different names, which made it harder to pin down.

"Please do," Pauline said. "If there is someone out to kill you, and I'm still not certain about that, you don't want to spur them into action. They've been very quiet for days now."

"That's because you never let me out of your sight," Alex said, "and I now stick to busy, public places."

With that Pauline had to be content. She jumped in her car and drove off, leaving Alex watching from the window. Alex's air of innocence was even more unsettling than her temper, Pauline decided, as she pulled out into the rush hour traffic.

Once she was sure Pauline was gone, Alex dressed and set out for the cousin's house. The last thing she intended to do was drink endless cups of tea while watching the house. Action was what she wanted and would have. The walk out of the village was bracing and set her up for the fight. When the morning rush was over, she'd pounce.

By ten o'clock, Alex thought it was time to make her move. She left the café, crossed the street and knocked on the door with the heavy walking stick she'd borrowed from Pauline's closet. Inside, she could hear the woman stirring and then footsteps approaching the door from the other side. It opened and the woman stood before her.

"Yes?" She asked.

"I'm Alexandra Wade," Alex replied.

"Yes?" the woman said again, in a more puzzled tone.

"I'm sure you know who I am and why I'm here," Alex said.

'I'm sorry, you must have the wrong house," the woman replied, even more puzzled. "Who is it you're looking for? Maybe I can help point you in the right direction."

"It's no use," Alex said. "I know who you are, and I know you're trying to kill me. Don't play games."

The woman looked alarmed and then a smile spread across her face. "This is that TV program, isn't it?" She said,

"I can't remember the name." Then, she beamed and leaned out to look around the corners of the wall, "Candid Camera, that's the one. Am I on now?"

"This is not a TV program," Alex said, growing flustered. "You're frightened I'll take your husband's share of the Cheney Trust and leave you all destitute."

The woman looked alarmed again. "I don't think this is very nice," she said. "I don't care if it is TV, I won't have it." She slammed the door shut.

Alex rapped on the door again. The woman appeared at the window and gestured for her to leave.

"I'm not going until you admit you're behind the attacks on my life," Alex shouted. She wished she'd thought to put her foot in the door while it had been open. Shouting through the window this way was embarrassing.

The woman opened the small pane at the top of the window and shouted. "I will call the police if you don't leave now."

"And I'll tell the police what I know," Alex yelled back. A small crowd was beginning to appear at doors and windows along the street.

"You're mad," the woman shouted. "Go away."

"I'm not mad," Alex shouted. "I'm the rightful heir and you'll lose your inheritance. That's the truth and that's why you're trying to kill me."

The woman, now apparently scared beyond caring what anyone thought, began calling for help from the neighboring houses.

A man detached himself from his doorway opposite and began to move toward Alex. Realizing she hadn't thought this through sufficiently, Alex quickly ran down the driveway and back along the lane to Whalley from where she'd come. She didn't stop running until she'd rounded a bend in the road and couldn't be seen by any potential pursuers. She stepped into a small, wooded area beside the road and waited. After a few minutes, she realized there were no pursuers. She returned to the road and walked home. Pauline would find this hilarious if she found out, but Pauline wasn't going to know.

The moment she was back at Pauline's house, Alex began packing. She was ready to leave when she saw Pauline's car pull into the drive.

Pauline was hardly through the door, when Alex said, "I'm going to London. You're right. I need to read that will properly for myself. I'll leave on the morning train. Can you give me a lift to the station?"

"Certainly, I can," Pauline said, removing her coat and hat. "Why the sudden rush?"

"I watched today, all day, and nothing happened," Alex lied, "and I came to realize examining that will is the only simple way to find out what this is about and who is doing these things."

"Will you be back tomorrow night, or will you stay until Thursday?"

"I think it would be safest to assume I might not find what I'm looking for right away tomorrow," Alex said. "I'll come back on Thursday."

"Can I suggest an alternative?" Pauline asked, somewhat hesitantly as she wasn't sure how Alex would react; she seemed so jumpy.

"I've made up my mind," Alex said.

"I was only going to suggest a one-day delay to your trip," Pauline said.

"Why?"

"You want to bring this to a close quickly, and I agree that would be best," Pauline said. "Here's what I suggest."

26

ALEX RETURNS TO LONDON

The train to London took forever but Alex didn't mind. Compared to her flight from Australia and the emotional rollercoaster of the past few days, it was restful; a relief that even the speculative glances of the soldiers drinking steadily in the far corner of the carriage couldn't spoil. She ignored them with practiced ease. Ignoring men was her chief talent and now she knew why. It was nature's way of protecting her from something she couldn't handle. Men? She couldn't even manage talking with a collection of elderly ladies and a willing volunteer. Though she'd never been in love, she'd now learned that sad song her mother would sometimes sing to herself was true. She, Alex, had been in love with the idea of aristocracy, though she'd told herself she wasn't, and now she'd lost the 'joy that was just a moment long' and could only look forward to the 'pain that lasts the whole life through'. She leaned her brow against the cold damp carriage window and shivered. How could Mum have lived all her adult life with such pain in her heart, even knowing the pain was of her own making? Alex shook herself to clear the gloom that thinking about her mother always brought on.

Pauline's idea of saying goodbye to all the people she'd met in Whalley had led to peculiarly touching scenes, which had both pleased and embarrassed her. She knew *she* would miss her new acquaintances but would never have believed they would miss her, yet many said they would.

Even Celia Ormiston, who she knew only as the organizer of Society events, but whom Pauline was most insistent must be told, expressed her sorrow at Alex's leaving. Celia promised to pass on Alex's thanks to the Society committee members and hoped Alex would have a wonderful trip back to Australia. Alex corrected her, saying she wasn't going home right away. She was going to Somerset House to do lots more researching, now she had developed a passion for it. Celia asked her to send any interesting information she might find to her so the Society could add it to their records.

The train began to slow as it approached London's Euston Station and Alex prepared to leave the warmth of the carriage for the wintry air outside.

London was cold and gray, overcast with a blustery wind that numbed her cheeks and fingers as she walked to her hotel. She wished it would do the same for her heart and head, where turmoil ruled the day, alternating between happiness and misery with brief wild tangents along the way. At the hotel reception, she was given her room key and told the main floor and restaurant were taken by a private party for the evening. She must eat early or go out. She unpacked in her small room overlooking the back of the hotel, then lay on her bed and slept.

When she woke, it was almost seven o'clock on a dark evening and her first thought was to put on the room's small

TV and vegetate, but her mother's stern teachings about sloth and self-pity soon asserted themselves. She was too late to eat in the hotel. She would go out and experience a little of London at night. The thought didn't thrill her; not at all the way just saying the name, London, had only weeks ago.

It was raining. It seemed like it was always raining, and it, too, no longer thrilled her. The pubs were noisy and crowded with workers drinking before heading home to the suburbs. Though the crowds seemed happy, it wasn't as she imagined it. Swinging London had been on everyone's tongue when she was younger, and this didn't seem to be it. It had an air of desperation, in her mind, of something not right. Everywhere in the Western world was suffering, she knew, the news talked of nothing else, and maybe it hit the big cities hardest. After looking into, and failing to enter, several pubs, she found a Chinese restaurant that was open and still quiet, preparing for the crush that would come later.

After her meal, she set off back to her hotel. It was too cold and wet for sightseeing and she thought how this same weather in the Lake District had raised her spirits while here it depressed them. Now that the commuters were on their buses and trains, the street was quieter with only a few people, heads down, umbrellas up, scurrying from one place of shelter to the next. Alex was happy to let the cold wind and rain wash her face. Slowly she began to recover the feeling of being fresh and new. Her old life was now fully behind her. All its dreams and hopes were gone. She was re-born and free of it all. Her spirits rose at this idea, she was a phoenix rising from its ashes.

Then she heard the footsteps. Her heart momentarily stopped. She struggled to breathe deeply. She steeled herself to be ready and yet not look behind. Ahead of her was a couple, walking under a large umbrella, facing each other in happy conversation. They looked safe, and as carefully as she dared, she increased her pace and closed the distance between herself and them. With people nearby, her nerves began to settle. *Now,* she thought, *how could I look around without seeming to?* Her dilemma was answered immediately. The woman pointed at something in a shop window, and they stopped.

Alex stopped too and pretended interest in the window's contents. From the corner of her eye, she saw a figure, aimlessly studying another window some twenty feet behind her on the street. Turning her head, she could see her hotel only five more walking minutes away.

"Excuse me," she said to the couple. "Are you going to the end of this street?"

They looked bemused at being addressed by a complete stranger or maybe they were so immersed in their own private world they were surprised to see her at all.

"We are," the man said. "Why?"

"I'm staying at the hotel there," Alex pointed to the brightly lit doorway, where guests to the party were now streaming in, "and I think that man behind me is following me. I'd like some company for the walk."

The man looked down the street. "If there was someone, he's gone," the man said, "but stay close. We'll walk with you."

ALEX FLEW UP the stairs to her room, threw off her wet coat and hat, and with trembling fingers called Pauline's number.

"Pauline," Alex whispered, when the phone was picked up, "is that you?"

"Of course, it's me," Pauline replied. "Who else would it be? Are you in London? Why are you whispering?"

"I'm in the hotel and I'm whispering because I'm frightened," Alex said. "You said I was to call if I saw I was being followed."

"That was quick," Pauline said, frowning. "I thought it would be a day or so. He's stolen a march on us, as they say in the military."

"What do I do?"

"You sit tight until I get there," Pauline said. She glanced at her watch. Would there be a night train to London, or would she have to get the first one out in the morning?

"What makes you think you're being followed?" Pauline asked, keeping Alex's mind from imagining the worst.

"Coming back to my hotel tonight, I heard footsteps behind me. Exactly like last time. I looked back and I saw a man I've seen around Whalley."

"Are you sure? It wasn't just someone who looked like someone?"

"I'm sure – and I think he knows I recognized him. Our eyes met and when I looked again, he was gone. Pauline, I'm really frightened."

"Call the local police," Pauline said.

"What can I say? I saw someone in London I saw a few days ago in Whalley?"

"If you tell them about the accident and the mugging, they'll understand."

"Those things happen all the time; they'll think I'm hysterical."

"They aren't allowed to think women are hysterical anymore. Phone them."

"You phone them. Phone Trevelyan," Alex said.

"I'm about to. In the meantime," Pauline said, "you

explain to the hotel front desk and get them to keep a close watch on your room. If I can't get a train tonight, I'll be on the first one in the morning."

"Thank you," Alex said gratefully. "Call me here as soon as you know." She gave Pauline her room number, the hotel address and hung up. She locked the door and put on the security chain but, looking at it again, it seemed pitifully inadequate. Any man could bust the door open. After wedging a chair under the door handle, Alex took Pauline's advice and alerted the front desk.

Pauline's call to the rail station confirmed the next train she could reasonably catch wasn't until five the following morning. Her next call was to Detective Trevelyan. She found him still at work.

"I'll have the local station look in on the hotel, Miss Riddell," Trevelyan said, "but I'm working tonight on an actual murder, which I don't think my superintendent will thank me for abandoning."

"I can't be there until tomorrow morning, Detective," Pauline said, "so anything you can do is appreciated."

After the train station and the police, Pauline called her London colleague, Jim. There was no answer. She left a message and went to pack.

As she was going to bed, Jim called back, by which time Pauline's frustration was at boiling point.

"Are you sure you read that will properly?" she demanded the moment she knew who it was.

"What?" Jim asked.

"The de Cheney will. Did you read it properly?"

"Of course, I did. Why?"

"Because Alex was knocked down by a car, then mugged," Pauline replied coldly, "and now she's being followed. There must be a connection."

"People are knocked down or mugged every day," Jim said.

"How many people do you know who have had either happen to them?" Pauline demanded. "I don't know one. And I certainly don't know of anyone but Alex who has had both happen!"

"Well," Jim began, her anger making him wary, "I was almost knocked down once."

"Everybody is almost knocked down once but hardly anyone is, that's my point," said Pauline savagely. "Now is there something I should know about that will?"

"You never told me about a mugging," Jim began. "And the accident was weeks ago, surely there's no connection. As for being followed, how does she know? These are dark winter nights and she's a visitor. We must all look the same to her."

"You can rationalize all you want," Pauline said. "Too much has happened in too short a time for this to be chance. And if Alex says there's a man following her and she's scared stiff, then I believe her. So, stop playing for time and answer me. Is there anything in that will I should know about?"

"Okay," Jim said, "I will." There was an air of triumphant gloating in his voice that chilled Pauline. "But first some history. You remember that meeting where we were laying out our different positions before the board?"

"What?" Pauline asked, before the memory of what she'd said that day hit her like a punch to the stomach. It had been shortly after joining the company. Jim was presenting and she, a newcomer, unaware of the difference in company culture, suggested an alternative solution that had already been discarded by the team. It derailed the meeting and led to some unpleasantness after.

"Well," Jim continued, "I swore then I'd pay you back someday. Well, this is the day."

"Jim, that was heat of the moment. I apologized. You can't have held it against me all these months," Pauline said.

"That exchange cost me dearly after, with my boss and with others," Jim replied. "You're good at your job, Pauline, we know that, but you'll find you have few friends when you need them."

As this was something Pauline herself thought often enough, she couldn't deny his words. "Okay," she said, "you're right about me but this isn't about me. It's about an Australian woman who was told she was an heiress, who now believes she isn't, but I now strongly suspect she is."

There was silence for a moment while Jim shifted gears. "All right. We're even now so I'll tell you. The trust was to go to, and I quote, a child born to Adelaide Fuller between the months of June and August 1945. If the child isn't found, and only if the child isn't found, do the proceeds go to the cousins and the Fund for Unmarried Mothers."

"You realize you've put Alex's life at risk by not telling me this?"

"I wasn't to know that," Jim said.

"I told you about the hit and run."

"But you never told me about a mugging," Jim retorted. "Tonight, is the first I've heard about that or her being followed. When you asked me to look into the will you said you just wanted to cover all the lines of enquiry. How was I to know someone was trying to kill her?"

"Okay, okay," Pauline said, "but you still shouldn't have done it. What if Alex had gone home without finding this out?"

"I was going to tell you, after you'd told her she wasn't an heiress," Jim said. "I just wanted you to look stupid, not rob the woman of what's rightfully hers."

"I won't forgive this, Jim," Pauline said. "You may think we're even, but I don't."

"Suit yourself, Pauline, but remember what I said about friends."

The phone went dead. Pauline replaced the handset. She'd many times realized that being a team member was as important as being good at your job. This small betrayal by her colleague showed her once again how her inability to make friends was harming her future, even though she hadn't been aware of it. Undercurrents, undetectable to her, were mapping out her career without her being able to defend herself. She shrugged. She could only do what she could and for the rest, it would shake itself out one way or another. However, she swore to herself, she would find a way to punish Jim because if it became known he'd injured her without retaliation, she wouldn't be safe from any of her colleagues.

27

DANGER IS NEAR

Alex peered through the spyhole in the door. Her heart leapt with relief when she saw Pauline's face staring back at her. She opened the door and tugged her inside.

"Thank God, you're here," Alex said.

"Nothing happened through the night?" Pauline asked, as she laid her case on the bed.

"No, nothing," Alex replied ruefully, "particularly not sleep."

Pauline grinned. "Fortune favors the brave," she said. "We're near the end."

"I remember you saying I probably wasn't really in any danger," Alex said, crossly. "Otherwise, I wouldn't have listened to your crazy advice."

"It's true," said Pauline, smiling. "Still, even then I cautioned you to take care."

"Actually, I was glad to phone you," Alex admitted. "When I heard the man following me and saw I recognized him, I was excited and scared all at the same time."

"Good because we need you to keep your nerve for this final part. Now, you're sure about this man?"

Alex shook her head. "I didn't make him up."

"What did he look like?"

"Let me think."

"You've had all night to think," Pauline said. "And you said you recognized him."

"But not to describe," Alex said, ignoring Pauline's jibe. "Well, he's a bit taller than average, his hair is black, graying at the temples, and he has a ponytail. He wears a jacket and white modern shirt, no collar or tie. Jeans and leather shoes, not trainers."

"Good," said Pauline, "but what does he look like? You've described his clothes, what about his face, posture, type? We need to have this straight. He can change his clothes."

Alex, who didn't see herself as a clothes-conscious woman, seemed inclined to be upset at this sarcastic question, but mastered her annoyance, and continued, "He's good-looking in a severe kind of way. He's well-off, slim, fit. Oh, and dark eyes and eyebrows, a lean face."

"All right. Anything else?"

Alex shook her head.

"Well, that will do for now," Pauline said. "Let me get myself settled and we'll go out for a walk. I need some exercise after that journey and, who knows, it may bring your mysterious admirer out into the open where I can see him."

"Don't joke," Alex said. "Whatever he is, he's not an admirer."

"I'm making light of it to keep our spirits up," Pauline said. "It's what I do when things look dark."

They walked the length of the street and through a nearby park, doing all they could to look as if they weren't scanning every man they saw, but the mystery man didn't appear. For Pauline, this day was strangely reminiscent of the days she'd spent with Poppy walking London's busy streets all those years before.

Losing her almost daily talks with Poppy was one of the worst things about her move to Lancashire. Now, they could only talk by phone and the long-distance charges were too expensive for daily chats. Without investigations or local gossip to share, it seemed, they also had little to talk about when they did call each other. As well, Pauline had to admit, Poppy had become rather odd in her habits. The determination to become a great reporter was taking its toll.

"You're very quiet, Pauline," Alex said.

"Sorry, I was thinking about life and the people who have come into, and drifted out of, mine."

"Do you mean me?"

Pauline laughed. "Not at all, though it probably sounded quite pointed to you. No, I was here in this park some years ago with someone else and I'd quite forgotten."

"Not a man, then," Alex said.

"No, not a man. A friend." Pauline roused herself to be more companionable. "It's growing dark, we should think about eating before we get back to the hotel."

They had an early dinner in a classier looking pub, noisy with city men loudly boasting about their latest financial coups, which Pauline recognized as the usual veneer to cover their desperation over their losses. Like all gamblers, they remembered only their winnings.

"Do you think they're always like this?" Alex asked.

"Yes," Pauline said bluntly. "The stock market is a place for people who can live on their nerves and yet thrive. To do that, though, you have to release the pent-up energy somewhere and the pub is the place to do it, at lunch and after the closing bell."

"Every day?" Alex said, perplexed.

"Different brokers on different days and times," Pauline said. "Stock markets have interests all around the world and some markets never close."

"Do your investigations get you involved with this?" Alex asked.

Pauline smiled. "Sometimes. We usually get called in when a company is teetering. And it's often because of the hyper-activity you see and hear right now because it's what alerts the authorities to the illegal behavior going on inside a company."

"So, you see this a lot," Alex said, almost shouting above the growing tumult.

"I don't personally," Pauline said. "I'm usually in a back-room trawling through the trail of documented destruction they leave behind."

"Is that what you were doing in Australia?"

"It's what I was doing, yes, but that wrongdoing wasn't brought to light by unusual share-dealings," Pauline said.

Alex stared at the men jostling around the bar, with more arriving by the minute. "They seem to be enjoying themselves," she said, as a tray of glasses crashed to the floor, raising a cheer from those not soaked in spilt beer.

"Desperation often looks like pleasure to those on the outside," Pauline replied, coldly eyeing another man with a tray who was jostling his way through the crowd and appeared heading straight for Pauline and Alex. He seemed to take the hint and veered off to her left toward a table of less rowdy drinkers.

"He isn't here," Alex said, misinterpreting Pauline's scanning of the room and anticipating her question.

"You're sure?"

"You'd think this would be a place for him to appear, but

I've looked carefully," Alex replied. "Maybe he's gone. Maybe I imagined it."

"I suspect you didn't," Pauline said. "Unusual things often appear for just a moment and we can't believe what we've seen after. But our senses are honed to keep us safe. If your senses say you saw him last night, then he's here some-where. Just not in this pub, maybe." She didn't add that the man may well be outside waiting for a less public place to strike; it would only make Alex even more nervous than she was now.

But even the walk back to their hotel was uneventful and, after a quiet evening reading, they retired to bed early.

28

PAULINE HUNTS HER PREY

P auline woke with a start, then relaxed. It was the same whenever she visited London. The early noises in the street were just the usual big city traffic. She rose from the armchair where she'd been resting and stretched the kinks out of her joints. She'd taken a room in the hotel but hadn't liked to leave Alex alone.

She crossed the floor to the bed and shook Alex awake. "We have to get up," Pauline said. "We have a long day of sightseeing and souvenir buying ahead of us."

"Do we have to?" Alex asked sleepily.

"You know we do. With luck the fellow stalking you will be watching, and he'll follow us. This time I can see him too and I have a better chance of recognizing him than you do."

"It has to be one of the cousins or that witch of a wife's bought and paid hitman," Alex said, wrapping herself in a bathrobe and heading for the bathroom, "but I still don't understand why. They of all people know I'm not going to inherit."

As Pauline had withheld the information about the true words of the will, Alex's statement didn't surprise her. In fact, until now, she'd decided it was better Alex remain in the dark to prevent her doing something outrageous. Now, however, Pauline thought, she should know a little more, so she'd understand the plan Pauline had set in motion.

"You're right," Pauline agreed, shouting through the bathroom door. "They should know the will, which reminds me of something I've been too busy to tell you these past few hours."

"I'm the rightful heir and I'm worth millions," Alex called back, somewhat sarcastically. She was too busy grooming to care much about some new twist to an old story.

"Maybe and maybe," Pauline replied.

"Well, I'm glad that's cleared up. For a moment I thought you knew something important."

"I heard from my contact yesterday the will wasn't as straightforward as he'd first thought," Pauline continued, ignoring her interruption. She decided to present Jim's revelation as new information, rather than deceit.

"Go on," Alex said, tying her bathrobe as she exited the bathroom.

"The principal beneficiary was a child born to Adelaide Fuller between June and August 1945, if he or she can be found."

Alex stopped dead in the center of the room. "Do you think that means me?" she asked incredulously.

"Doesn't it?"

"Wow," she said. "I think it does."

"What I don't understand," Pauline continued, "is why Jocelyn didn't look for Adie when he came back. Or, if he did, why he couldn't find her?"

After a moment's thought, Alex said indignantly, "You don't listen to a word I say, do you? I told you why days ago."

She folded her arms, tapped her foot on the floor ominously and glared at her.

"Okay, okay," Pauline laughed. "Tell me again."

"No. You're the expert. I'm just the hopeless amateur who keeps getting it wrong," Alex simpered mockingly.

Pauline frowned. "I never said that—" she began.

"You didn't have to. I said it for you."

"And now you've said it, please enlighten me further."

"Mum called herself de Cheney on her marriage certificate to George Wade," Alex said. "Sir Jocelyn, or whoever he used to do the work, would have been looking for Adelaide Fuller and she'd ceased to exist."

Pauline nodded. "I think you're right. Though why he didn't think of the possibility she would be using his family name, I don't know."

"Because they weren't married, maybe not even officially engaged, and he thought her an honorable woman," Alex said. "To someone like him, what she did would have been unthinkable."

Pauline laughed. "Maybe," she said, "but maybe it was just he hired private investigators and told them to look for Adelaide Fuller and her using his name never occurred to him. You have to get over your anger at your mother someday, you know."

Alex grimaced. "I will in time, I guess. Everyone does, don't they?"

"Don't ask me," Pauline said. "I'm still liable to throttle my mother every time I'm home for more than a weekend."

"Is that why you spent Christmas with me?"

Pauline shook her head. "No," she said. "I'd already decided to get away for the holiday this year. I thought a hotel in Scotland would be the perfect spot to see in the New Year in true Scottish fashion. You saved me from that."

"Sorry," Alex said. "I was so wrapped up in my own affairs, I never thought you might have plans."

"Don't worry," Pauline said. "The others I was going with did very well without me. I'm never the life of the party, even on my good days. Now, we need to get out into the open where your mysterious friend is hoping to strike, we need to give him the opportunity to do it."

"It sounds an odd thing to say," Alex said, "but I hope he does attack soon. The suspense is killing me."

Pauline laughed. "Here's hoping that is just a figure of speech."

"The will does finally confirm mother's story about a wedding, or probably even and engagement, was a lie," Alex said. "The will says Adelaide *Fuller*."

Pauline nodded. "It seems Jocelyn was an honorable man even in that," she said.

"I only hope I am his child," Alex said. "I wouldn't put it past my mother to trap him that way."

"He thought so," Pauline said. "That's all that matters now."

"I'M sick of looking at stuff." Pauline, never a shopper, complained to Alex who was looking at brushes, combs, and other grooming items all marked *London* and sporting a picture of Big Ben. They'd wandered the streets and the visitor stores all morning and afternoon, returning often to the hotel and always watching and waiting.

"I'm buying you a gift," Alex said, as she'd said in the jewelry stores, clothes stores, and every gift shop they'd seen.

"You don't have to," Pauline said, which had been her unvarying reply.

"I don't," Alex replied, "but I want to. If it wasn't for you, I'd be returning to Australia in a day or two thinking mum's whole story was a lie, and not just parts of it."

Pauline looked about hoping for a glimpse of a familiar face. The shop assistants were busy elsewhere and the floor was emptying as it grew nearer closing time but there was still no one who looked like the description Alex had given her. He'd know how much he'd stand out in this very female section of the store, Pauline thought tiredly.

"This new information still may not get you anything," Pauline said. "The charity and the cousins have been living off the de Cheney Trust for twenty years now. I doubt there's much left."

"I don't really care now," Alex replied. "Just knowing mum didn't put me through all of that hurt based on a delusion and a pack of lies is enough. Now, I just feel guilty about what I've called her, what I thought about her. Somehow, knowing she wasn't quite what I thought she was is enough."

"You weren't to know," Pauline countered. "The evidence—"

"You didn't jump to wicked conclusions," Alex interjected. "I did."

"My views weren't colored by knowing your mother."

"Even when you said I was letting my prejudice sway me, I still kept right on cursing her," Alex said grimly. "If I could do this to someone who spent her life trying to do her best for me..." she broke off and then after a moment, added, "Well, I'll just have to be careful to do better in the future." Blushing lightly, Alex turned quickly away before Pauline could answer and marched off to the till.

While Alex was waiting to pay for her purchase, Pauline pretended to examine a rack of London-themed head scarves. She considered Alex's outburst, turning the words over and over in her mind. It was the pendulum swinging too far on the side of guilty that made her feel uneasy. Sure, Alex had said some harsh things about her mother, so what? Everyone does. She'd thought some unpleasant things about all the members of her family throughout the years and she didn't feel the least bit guilty. She shrugged. Sooner or later, Alex would settle back to somewhere in the middle. People always did. Then she would see things straight.

Pauline glanced at Alex, standing in the short line at the till. Alex was gazing at the woman ahead of her with a strange intensity, considering they were only a foot apart, but Pauline could see Alex was signaling with her eyes and mouthing some words, silently imploring her to approach.

As she drew near, Pauline heard Alex whisper, "Don't look right away but slowly look over to the men's jackets on my left. He's there."

Pauline returned to where she'd been examining the head scarves and pretended to decide between a blue and red one. As she did so, from the corner of her eye she observed the man Alex had pointed out. He was turned the wrong way to see his face so, choosing the blue scarf, she wandered slowly back to join Alex at the till. Now she could see him: tanned, forties, receding hair that was thick enough at the back for a short ponytail. He looked successful, moneyed, and cruel. His dark eyes, aquiline nose, and thin lips suggested a man used to being the boss. She knew him at once.

"You don't recognize him?" Pauline whispered.

"He's neither of the cousins," Alex said, "and he isn't the witchy wife, sadly. I wanted it to be her."

"All of them could be in this," Pauline said. "It could be a group effort and this man could just be the instrument of their anger."

"What are we going to do?"

"Go back to the hotel, keeping to the busy public places and re-think," said Pauline. She needed to re-think because she did recognize the man and it confirmed what she'd learned. Alex hadn't asked if Pauline recognized the man, and this was too public a place to tell her.

29

HUNTER OR HUNTED?

It was time. Alex looked out of the window into the street, where streetlamps and lighted windows showed a handful of people and cars making their way homeward late on this Friday evening. Outside the window, London seemed to be at home, settling down for dinner before for coming out for the night. She slipped on her coat, combed her hair, placed her hat carefully, and nodding to Pauline, who smiled encouragingly, took a deep breath and left her room. She took the elevator to the lobby, crossed it and pushed open the hotel's heavy doors. Friday the Thirteenth seemed a good night for risking her life, Alex thought, as she set out on the short walk to the evening service at the church across the park.

Outside, the evening air was fresh, frosty even, and it nipped her nose and cheeks. Alex walked quickly. The service was at seven. She had plenty of time but being out alone made her nervous. Crossing the now almost empty street, Alex entered the small park opposite, which lay between their hotel and the church she'd chosen. Londoners weren't churchgoers anymore, it seemed, despite all the churches they had to choose from. She was the only person on the pathway that led directly to the church, where she could see lights shining dimly through stained-glass windows. Tall bushes lining the narrow path made her feel queasy inside, but she dismissed that. What were the chances her admirer, as Pauline called him, was waiting around the park on the off chance she would come this way alone? She was more likely to be hit by lightning in punishment for missing church than being attacked by the hitman of aggrieved heirs.

Her footsteps echoed on the hard ground. Somewhere nearby she could hear a man with a dog. That was re-assuring; witnesses were always handy. Not that they were needed, she reminded herself severely, because no hitman was anywhere nearby. The villain was in a low dive of a bar drowning his frustration at her always being safe from him.

It was the faintest of movements, just a flash of something even darker than the shadows among the trees behind her right shoulder, but it was enough to set her heart thumping. She picked up the pace, her heels tock, tock, tocking faster on the hard pavement. The sound made her more frightened. If she was being pursued, he would know she'd seen him and he might attack sooner, thinking she might escape. Summoning all her willpower she slowed her pace back to a brisk walk. The slow pounding ache in her head, that had been the bane of her life after he'd hit her last time, returned. A slow, pulsing ache that started at the back and rolled through her brain to an intense crescendo behind her forehead.

The man with the dog was comfortably close as Alex entered an even more thickly wooded part of the path. She looked about nervously; it would be here or not at all. When this gloomy evergreen patch was done, the path was open all the way to the road and the church opposite. A rustling branch was all the warning she needed, Alex yelled, "Help," and pressed the alarm in her pocket. Its wailing screech stopped the man in his tracks. Then, realizing there was no going back, he leapt at her, the silvery flash of a knife blade foremost.

Alex, given time to act by his momentary hesitation, dodged the blade and ran back along the path, almost knocking over the black and tan blur of a German shepherd dog that raced past her. Man and dog collided behind her in a snarling flurry of arms and legs that ended when the burly dog handler arrived and grabbed the man's wrist. Almost contemptuously, the dog handler flicked the knife aside. The man was screaming abuse when another policeman arrived to pin him to the ground and handcuff him.

"You sure you're up to this?" Pauline asked, as Alex drank the police canteen's hot sweet tea, recommended by the desk sergeant as a preventative for shock.

"I'm fine, really," Alex said. "I'm on tenterhooks waiting to hear who this lunatic is but otherwise, I'm fine. I've never had so much excitement in my life."

"Few people do," Pauline said, "and they like it that way."

"Wimps," snorted Alex. "I wouldn't have missed this for anything."

"How are you going to get through the rest of your life?" Pauline laughed, awestruck by Alex's fierce expression and shining eyes.

"I'm thinking of becoming a private detective," Alex said. "What do you think?"

"I think you're mad," Pauline replied, "but I can see how going back to an ordinary office life might be difficult."

"Miss Wade, Miss Riddell," the sergeant's voice boomed down the narrow corridor, "could you come in here, please?" He pointed to a door beside him.

Alex and Pauline entered the room, which was dark except for one dimly lit window that showed the man who attacked Alex being interviewed by Detective Trevelyan and another man.

"Do you recognize him?" the sergeant asked Alex.

"Only as the man who attacked me," said Alex. "We're pretty confident we know who he's working for but we're hoping you were going to confirm it."

"His name is Nicholas Harrison. Does that mean anything to you?"

"No," said Alex, "should it? He isn't one of the cousins, that I do know."

"I think Miss Riddell here can help you there," said the sergeant.

"Pauline?" Alex said, puzzled.

"Nicholas Harrison is the lawyer for the de Cheney Fund for Unmarried Mothers. He's been embezzling the trust's funds for a decade or so now," Pauline said.

"But how did he know about me?" Alex asked, puzzled at this completely new addition into her world of potential enemies.

"Your arrival caused quite a stir up there in Ashton," Pauline said. "He heard about you and your claim from one of the ladies of the Historical Society. Not that the woman knew what she was saying, if you follow my meaning, she didn't know he was embezzling from the fund and your claim would bring it all out into the open. I saw him that first time I went to the Society's meeting, though I didn't know who he was then. He wisely didn't introduce himself when everyone else did."

"Then I'm lucky the two cousins are honest men," said Alex with a shudder. "I could have had three angry dispossessed men after me."

"If you don't need us anymore," Pauline said to the sergeant, "I think we should go." She wrapped her arm around Alex protectively and walked her away.

"Maybe I won't become a private detective, after all," said Alex sadly, as they entered the hotel lobby, ignoring the interested stares of everyone who'd seen them arrive in a police car. "I never even thought of that."

"Probably a wise decision," Pauline said. "It takes practice and patience, something you're not good at."

"How did you think of it?"

"It was Jim who set me on the right path," Pauline said. "I told you. Remember?"

"No," said Alex curtly, not interested in anything Jim might have said. "I'm going to have a drink. I've been teetotal up to now but drinking calms the nerves for people in fiction so I hope it will work for me in real life. What are you going to do?"

"I'll come with you," Pauline said after a pause. "Just to be sure you're safe. You know what happens when you go out alone. And I think I may join you in a drink, too. This time, tea seems inadequate."

"It wasn't you who was the bait," Alex said, laughing.

"That's what made it worse," Pauline said. "Sending someone to their possible death or mutilation isn't in my nature. I could never be an officer in the army."

"You never said anything about death or mutilation that I recall," Alex said, laughing.

"I didn't want you to say yes to prove your courage to

me," Pauline replied. "I wanted a calm decision, not bravado."

The elevator stopped and the doors opened. Pauline ushered Alex out.

As they walked down the corridor, Alex asked, "Do you think I will really inherit?"

Pauline, who was fumbling in her bag for the room key took a moment to answer. "I've no idea," she said. "It still seems a long shot to me. I guess we'll know tomorrow when the lawyers are open."

"It's just I'd like to stay here in England, and I don't know if I could without the money," Alex said.

"Fifteen minutes to freshen up," Pauline said, "and then we hit the bar. Isn't that what they say?"

THE HOTEL'S bar was busy, but Detective Trevelyan had no trouble finding them.

"Good evening, Detective," Pauline said, as he approached. "Pull up a chair, if you can find one."

"I won't stay," he said, "I just came to tell you Mr. Harrison has confessed to both the attacks on Miss Wade and the embezzlement. I think he was rather relieved it was all over."

"Not as much as I am," Alex said, indignantly.

Trevelyan laughed. "I can understand your lack of sympathy, Miss Wade," he said. "I imagine I'd feel the same way."

"Why was he doing it?" Pauline asked.

"Oh, the usual," Trevelyan said. "A lifestyle he wanted but couldn't afford and a small but expensive drug habit. I think it began small and was growing worse."

"Yes," Pauline said, nodding. "I knew as soon as I saw the

dropping off in the annual cashflow to the charity. He took almost every penny of the money last year. This year he'd have taken it all."

"Your friend Inspector Ramsay was right about you," Trevelyan said. "I'm glad I trusted his judgment. Goodbye, Miss Riddell, Miss Wade. Have a safe return trip home, wherever that may be."

"I live in Lancashire now, detective," Alex said, grinning. "I'm moving there tomorrow."

They watched the detective wriggle his way through the crowd and out of sight.

"You've decided to take up your inheritance then?" Pauline asked. "The weather hasn't put you off."

"It felt like home the day I got off the train in Preston," Alex said. "I can't explain it. It just is. And the weather is wonderful. I won't hear a word said against it."

30

AFTERMATH

"Pauline," Alex asked, as they sipped tea in the local teashop where Alex met her group of friends most days. "Do you think I did the right thing in agreeing to let the cousins keep their share of the inheritance?"

The days since returning from London had been spent in lawyers' offices discussing the will and what Alex's arrival meant for the existing beneficiaries. The shell of a charity that the Fund for Unmarried Mothers had long since become was to be wound up and the law office that Harrison was a partner in had agreed to pay compensation outside of court. A very satisfactory arrangement in Pauline's opinion.

"Yes, I do," Pauline replied. "Why?"

"I don't know, it's a lot of money, I guess. And buying my house before the lawyer's insurance company has paid up, was that wise?"

"They've agreed to pay, in writing," Pauline murmured. "And in writing is a big deal with lawyers. The bank was happy to give you a mortgage on the strength of it. Stop worrying."

"You know I still don't see how you pieced it all together."

Pauline made a face, unsure whether she would be safe to let her guard down by admitting to her many wrong turns. She shrugged, after all it wasn't like she and Alex would have much to do together in the future. They would be moving in such different social circles.

"Well," Pauline began, "as I told you, Jim's comment about how unmarried mothers weren't in need of assistance nowadays piqued my interest. For the first time, I saw a twist to the motive. Now you're not allowed to tell anyone this next piece, but I saw Harrison at the Historical Society meeting long before and I didn't like him. To be honest, I just knew if there was anything bad going on in all of this, he'd be at the bottom of it."

"Just a hunch, then."

"I prefer an educated guess based on my years of experience of wrongdoing and wrongdoers," Pauline said a little defensively.

"Well, I won't tell anyone, so your secret is safe with me. Your reputation as a dogged, analytical pursuer of the truth will remain intact."

31

A NEW BEGINNING?

The phone on Pauline's desk rang. Monday morning, the very moment she'd sat down. Couldn't they wait, she thought, even a few moments to let a body catch her breath? She picked up the handset.

"Yes," she said, tersely.

"Good morning, Pauline," Margaret, her boss's secretary, said, "how was your weekend?"

"Hello, Margaret," Pauline replied. "It was good, thanks. Very restful."

"I'm pleased to hear it because he has a new assignment for you."

"And it couldn't wait until a more reasonable hour?" Pauline asked.

"He's been waiting since last Friday night, right after you left the office," Margaret said. "You're lucky he didn't call you at home."

"It must have been a New Year's resolution on his part, was it?" Pauline asked. Despite her cynicism, she was intrigued. "And what is this assignment?"

"I'm not telling you. He'd murder me," Margaret said, laughing, "but I think you might like it."

"Now I'm terrified," Pauline said. "I think I'll go home sick."

"Five minutes," Margaret said, "and don't be late or he'll burst with frustration."

Pauline could hear Margaret's laughter as she put the phone down. It was intriguing but it sounded suspicious. Margaret wasn't a woman who played games or pranks and she never laughed at work. Feeling as though she was going to the scaffold, Pauline left her desk and made her way to the managing director's office.

Margaret was still smiling when Pauline arrived. "Can't you tell me anything?" Pauline asked.

Margaret pressed the intercom. "Miss Riddell is here, sir," she said, and when she heard the gruff, "send her in," she signaled Pauline to enter.

"Come in, Pauline," the MD said as she entered the office.

This is bad, Pauline thought, he never calls anyone by their given name.

"Take a seat, please," her boss said, pointing to the large leather chairs opposite him.

Pauline did, still wary, but growing amused at this obvious attempt to win her over before he'd even made the proposal. Whatever Margaret might think, her boss wasn't sure she was going to take the assignment and that was good. It would give her negotiating room.

"Did Margaret tell you why I wanted to see you?"

"She said you had a new assignment for me," Pauline said. There was no need to suggest Margaret thought she'd like it.

"Ah, good," he said. "How does Australia for six months sound?"

Pauline said, "I've just come back from there."

"And you liked it out there, I remember you saying."

"I would like to see more of the country," Pauline agreed.

"Your work was well regarded by the board out in Lithgow," her boss said. "They've asked if you would take the Finance Director position for a temporary period, say six months, and implement the recommendations from the report you and Entwhistle prepared for them. What do you think?"

Pauline wasn't entirely sure what to think. She'd hardly had time to furnish the house she'd bought months before. She hadn't even made it her own yet, she'd been so busy working. Worse, six months away might lose her ground in the intensely competitive office they all worked in. But six months to put in place an organization that would withstand future embezzlers was an opportunity people weren't often given. And the weather would be warmer. Australia was now in its summer season.

"Tell me about the job," Pauline said, "and I'll tell you what I think."

"You'll have practically a free hand," her boss said, "and they're offering a very generous living allowance on top of your regular salary. If you like it, you could probably negotiate your way into the position permanently."

Pauline returned home that evening and wandered around her house, almost in a dream. What to pack and what to put in storage? It seemed traitorous to the poor house to abandon it when she'd only just arrived back, but such was life. She wouldn't rent it out, tenants were so unreliable, but she'd arrange for someone to come in frequently enough to keep it nice.

Australia. Sunshine and the Outback. A new world. Hers to explore for the next six months, at least.

BONUS CONTENT

Here's an excerpt from my next book in the series: Then There Were Two...Murders?

Chapter 1: Newcastle-upon-Tyne, England, December 1953

Pauline stared at the letter in her hand, hardly daring to believe it possible. Only minutes ago, she'd been wondering how she could change her life to make something more exciting of it and here it was. A letter from a woman, Mrs. Elliott, who wanted her help and all because she'd been mentioned in the newspapers as having solved a murder when the police had given up. If it wasn't for the letter, which she could clearly see and feel in her hand, she'd have thought herself in a dream. A dream from which she'd wake and be disappointed.

She held up the letter so she could see it better in the light streaming through the window from the nearby street-light. The words seemed to float on the page, drawing her in.

'Dear Miss Riddell,

I saw the article in the Herald yesterday and your

amazing success in unmasking those killers. I have a puzzle
the police won't look at, but somebody should. I thought,
hoped, you might like to. I can't pay very much, I'm not rich
but it may interest you. It's not a serious thing like murder
but it is puzzling, and it worries me. Sorry if you think I'm
rambling. I just can't get it out of my mind. Maybe it would
be better if I explained a little, then you'd see.

First, you should know I live in an old house on the
outskirts of Mitford. It's very quiet, or at least it was.
Recently, I've heard noises, particularly at night. I have a
good security alarm system and I lock up carefully, so I don't
believe I'm in any danger. However, something is going on.

A week ago, I was crossing a stream on my daily walk by
a bridge I've used every day, twice a day, since I retired.
There's never been any trouble. On this occasion, the bridge
had come loose and it tipped me into the stream. Fortunately, though I'm old, I'm not frail and while I'm cut and
bruised, I'm not seriously hurt. But I could have been. I
showed the bridge to the police and told them about the
noises, but our local policeman man says the bridge is old
and the bad weather has driven a lot of animals to find
shelter in and around houses. What he said is true, but it
doesn't explain it. I've lived in this house nearly forty years
now and I know every creak – and so does Jem, my dog.

I have more to tell you, however, you may not be interested. If you are, please phone me at this number and I'll
explain more fully.

Yours Sincerely,
Doris Elliott

Pauline put down the letter and walked to the window,
where the cold December night was lit by the lights of
houses opposite and a nearby streetlamp. She told herself

she wanted to think about this invitation. Should she raise this woman's hopes and then dash them because she couldn't provide answers or because the answers were as ordinary as the local policeman said? She shook herself. What on earth was she thinking of? Of course, she'd phone and accept the cry for help. After all, it wasn't just Mrs. Elliott who needed her to use her gifts, she needed to use them as well. The new life she'd wondered about was stretching out before her. There could be no question about turning away. She glanced at her watch. It was too late to call now. She'd phone Mrs. Elliott after church in the morning.

If this excerpt has whetted your appetite for more, you can pre-order the book Then there Were Two... Murders?

If you can't wait to read more of Miss Riddell's adventures, you can find them here:

Starting with the first book in the series, In the Beginning, There Was a Murder

Or the second published book in the Miss Riddell Cozy Mystery series, It's Murder, On a Galapagos Cruise

Or the third published book of the series, A Murder for Christmas

Finally, if you know someone who would prefer a *Large Print* copy, here it is: In the Beginning, There Was a Murder

MORE OF MY BOOKS

You can find more books by P.C. James and Paul James here:

P.C. James Author Page: https://www.amazon.com/P.-C.-James/e/B08VTN7Z8Y

Paul James Author Page: https://www.amazon.com/-/e/B01DFGG2U2

GoodReads: https://www.goodreads.com/author/show/20856827.P_C_James

NEWSLETTER

To be kept up-to-date on everything in the world of Miss Riddell Cozy Mysteries, sign up to my Newsletter here.

DEDICATION

For my family. The inspiration they provide and the time they allow me for imagining and typing makes everything possible. I'd also like to thank my editors, illustrator and the many others who have helped with this book. You know who you are.

COPYRIGHT

ABOUT THE AUTHOR

I've always loved mysteries, especially those involving Agatha Christie's Miss Marple. Perhaps because Miss Marple reminded me of my aunts when I was growing up. But Christie never told us much about Miss Marple's earlier life. When writing my own elderly super-sleuth series, I will trace her career from the start. As you'll see, if you follow the Miss Riddell Cozy Mysteries over the coming years.

However, this is my Bio, not Miss Riddell's, so here goes with all you need to know about me: After retiring, I became a writer and, as a writer, I spend much of my day staring at the computer screen hoping inspiration will strike. I'm pleased to say it generally does — eventually. For the rest, you'll find me running, cycling, walking, and taking wildlife photos wherever and whenever I can. My cozy mystery series begins in northern England because that was my home growing up and that's also the home of so many great cozy mysteries. Stay with me though because Miss Riddell loves to travel as much as I do and the stories will take us to many different places around the world.

Made in the USA
Monee, IL
12 July 2021

73476561R00125